THE MAFIA AND
JONNY BLUE

THE MAFIA AND
JONNY BLUE

Chuck Hughes

 iUniverse®

THE MAFIA AND JONNY BLUE

iUniverse books may be ordered through booksellers or by contacting:

iUniverse
1663 Liberty Drive
Bloomington, IN 47403
www.iuniverse.com
844-349-9409

ISBN: 978-1-6632-2091-2 (sc)
ISBN: 978-1-6632-2115-5 (e)

Print information available on the last page.

iUniverse rev. date: 04/08/2021

PRELUDE ITALY 1920S

The world was already in turmoil before the Bolsheviks turned Russia into the USSR. Three years later, the fascist-egalitarian strike in Italy brought Benito Mussolini to power, putting all of Italy in an uproar. Eventually, the collapse of the fascist- egalitarian strike failed. That strengthened his reign. Being neutral in WWI enhanced his climb to enhancing a fascist government with him leading the National Fascist Party. Shortly after the end of WWI, he was on his way to being the youngest prime minister of Italy. It was not long before he became Italy's fascist dictator. While he did not survive WWII, the Mafia did.

While fascism prevailed, Luigi and Laura Milano were celebrating the birth of their only child, Mario. Like many others, he had a distaste for fascism and eventually drifted into the United States along with Alonzo Vallario, his wife, his son, and the Calabrese family. Both the Milano family and the Calabrese family settled in New York's ethnic Italian enclave in the Bronx. Alonzo Vallario found New York City more to his liking.

Mario grew up in poverty and avoided having the cost of raising a child. However, things didn't go the way he planned. In 1948, at the age of thirty, his son, Jonny, was born. It was in the Bronx that the Calabreses were also blessed with a son, Leonardo. Jonny and Leonardo became close friends.

"Leonardo's too hard to spell," Jonny said. "I think *Linny* is better." The nickname stuck. Unlike Jonny, Linny Calabrese was reckless and was introduced to the numbers racket and fed off of the poor Italian neighborhood. Little did they know they would eventually graduate to greater opportunities, Linny, after spending several years in prison for robbery, and Jonny, after enlisting in the Navy.

Mario still found it difficult to find a job that paid enough to feed his family. "I know a guy that can help you," one of his friends said. Mario was desperate and did not hesitate when Don Alonzo Vallario offered him a job in the Vallario *Business*. However, it didn't take long for him to see the risks in his new job. When he decided to get out, he learned that there was *no getting out*. The rackets made him a perfect fit in the Calabrese *Business*. At first, Mario was doing minor things for the business, but as he matured, his role became more hazardous. It was then he made a promise that he would be the last Milano to be involved with the Mafia. However, this was a pledge providence would not let him keep.

CHAPTER 1

The wind bristled through the evergreens, bringing with it a promise that winter was fading and spring was just around the corner. Like many things, the weather is often fallible and ambiguous. However, while other broken promises and covenants often demand penalties when they break their promises, the weather is formidable and free of retribution. Today, there would be a penalty.

Mafia Don Vallario, short in stature while abundant in body, with drooping jaws, dark shadows beneath ice-cold eyes, and steel-gray hair, spent the night deciding how he would get the money Nicky Greco owed him. He rarely discussed *business* in his 2 million dollar home in Manhattan, but losing sleep over the Greek made today an exception. Even muddle-minded Frenchie Durand knew there was a problem when he was summoned to the island mansion.

"Durand, I'm tired of dealing with the Greek," Vallario said while eating his three-egg omelet and palm-size fried sausage paddy breakfast, followed by a mouthful of coffee tainted with Jonny Walker Platinum whiskey.

After wiping the sausage grease from his thick lips, he gazed out the large dining room window at the long-legged blonde pulling herself out of the heated blue-water pool. She waved at him as she wrapped herself in a long towel. Vallario waved back, smiled, then returned to the last few bites of his sausage and Frenchie Durand.

"How much short was he this time, Boss?" Durand asked.

"How much?" Vallario said in his apathetic tone. "It's not an issue of *how much*. A dollar's too much. It's about respect. He's gotta learn that nobody disrespects me."

"You want me to take care of it?"

"Sending you to take care of the son-of-a-bitch was my plan, but—"

Durand interrupted him "If I was you, Boss, I'd send Paulie with me. It's time he got his hands dirty with some of the rough stuff. We'll give the Greek a lesson he won't forget."

The Don ignored Durand's interruption, something that would normally result in more than a gruff threat instead he just pointed his stubby finger at the bald giant he depended on when punishment was needed. "*Mister Durand*, you're not me . . . don't ever forget that. As for Paulie, he is a bit wimpy, but he has value; value you wouldn't understand."

"Sorry, Boss, I'll take care of the problem," Durand said, now eager to do the job. "It might take a little roughing up, but he'll get your message. If he don't, just tell me how deep you want him. I always got a shovel in my car."

"Six feet, when I called you," Vallario replied as he bit the tip-off of a Cuban cigar and spit it on the floor. "But I decided to give the Greek one more chance. Who knows, he might have had a run of luck with the cards. Anyway, seeing you at his doorstep would send him into hiding, or worse, running to the feds for protection. I can't take that chance. Instead, I'll use the carrot instead of the stick . . . for now. So, I'm going to send Jonny." Seeing the confusing look on Durand's face, Vallario shook his head. "You have no idea what the *carrot* and *stick* metaphor means do you?"

Durand hesitated then shook his head. "What's a meta . . .?"

"Let me explain it another way. A gentle voice can be very valuable at times." Vallario paused then continued. "Jonny B's the gentle voice—the carrot. If that doesn't get results, then I'll send you—the stick."

Durand nodded and smiled. "Ya, I get it. It's best to send the college boy with his carrot. Then later, send me with the stick to make the Greek see how serious his stupidity was."

Vallario pointed a finger at Durand again. "Yeah, that's what I mean. I'll tell you when and what to do if I need you. For now, all you have to do is tell Jonny to pay the Greek a visit."

"Boss, you know that blue-eyed Italian don't like me. Can I tell Paulie to call him?"

"Durand, no one likes you but everybody's scared of you. That's what I pay you for. All you have to do is find Paulie, and tell him to take my message to Jonny. Think you can do that?"

Durand nodded. "I got the carrot and stick meta . . . thing."

❖ ❖ ❖

It took several phone calls for Paulie to reach Jonny. "The Greek pissed the boss off again," he said when Jonny finally answered the phone.

"What has he done now, spit on the sidewalk?"

"It's more like he spit in his face."

Jonny shook his head. "It's about the missing money again, right?"

"If you listen to Vallario, everything is about *respect*, but it always boils down to money," Paulie said. "It's best to remember that."

Jonny shook his head. "If he wants me to go to him again, it's a waste of my time. Nicky doesn't have the money, and he can't get the money. Even if he could, he'd blow it away before Vallario ever got any of it."

"We all know Greco's not very bright, but—"

"Paulie, Vallario knew that when he pulled him out of the gutter."

"But he didn't know the Greek was a chiseler hooked on gambling," Paulie said. "Anyway, he needed him then."

"Apparently, he doesn't need him anymore. I can move money around for him, but I can't make Greco come up with money he doesn't have and is not likely going to have," Jonny said as he continued flipping through his books. "The boss should just write off the debt and shove Greco back to the slums where he came from."

"It doesn't work that way, Jonny," Paulie said. "It's not like the time I didn't count the drug money like I should have then let those damn Mexicans cheat me."

"That was stupid, too," Jonny said with a grin.

"Go ahead and laugh, but you don't know what it's like to count drug money with killer dope dealers staring at you while Homeland Security cops are staring down at you from their swirling helicopters!"

"That was *drug* money?" Jonny asked with a smirk. "I thought it was a donation to the boss's favorite charity, or so the books said."

"That's what you're for--making the books look right. Call it what you want, but coming up short with *Office* money isn't like just getting a parking ticket. Penalty for the parking ticket is usually just a warning." Paulie ran his hand across his neck, "But stealing the whole car!"

"Your shortage was only a few grand. Hiding a few thousand dollars out of an account with millions wasn't very hard to do. Besides, that was a one-time favor."

"That was a lifetime favor to me, Jonny. You put your ass on the line. If you hadn't fixed the books, I'd be in the same shit the Greek's in. I'll never forget that."

"Greco's a thief and an asshole on top of it, so why doesn't he send Durand to get his attention. He's hanging around doing nothing, while I'm up to my neck negotiating with those Mexicans."

"Greco isn't as stupid as people think . . . well, stealing from the boss was stupid," Paulie said with a laugh, "But if he sees Durand's ugly face, he might think he's going to . . . you know."

"Kill him?" Jonny said. "Not likely over a few grand."

"It's not a few grand, Jonny. He owes at least sixty large, maybe more. But to Vallario, it's not about the money, it's about loyalty."

"Paulie, I assure you, money has more pull than loyalty."

"You're probably right. Still, he doesn't want Greco to get scared and go to the feds spilling what he knows in exchange for protection."

Jonny laughed. "Maybe that's something we all should consider."

"That's not funny. Just don't let anyone hear you say that. As for the Greek, he's a bit jumpy already. Vallario figures he won't panic and run when he sees you. That's why he wants you to talk to him. You got that *gentle touch*."

Jonny shook his head in frustration. "Paulie, just because I have a few years of college and a soft Georgia accent doesn't necessarily mean I'm gentle! In fact," Jonny said with a smile, "I'm not any gentler than you or Durand. I just believe that sometimes asking can be more productive than demanding."

"Jonny, this isn't negotiable. The boss wants the Greek in his office by tomorrow . . . with the money!"

※———◆◆———※

Seventeen-year-old Nicholas Greco was a man in looks but a child in thinking. The lean, six-foot-tall, boy with coal-black hair was a product of the Bronx and Harlem Park. Mother died leaving him with an alcoholic father, which did little to curb his urge to eat from the hands of others. The hand that first fed him came from a forty-year-old prostitute. Fifty cents was his cut when he guided men to her pay-by-the-day room. He also learned about heroin from her. His teacher's overdose left him without an income, but that didn't last long. He soon moved from the Bronx to scouring Harlem's Needle Park, pushing heroin for his twenty-one-year-old boss. This kept his ego fed and money in his pocket. By the age of twenty-five, he had climbed the loan shark ladder of success and was another draft by Mafia Don, Alonzo Vallario. He had finally found another place where he fit, and it wasn't long before he became known as Nicky the Greek.

⬥ ◆ ◆ ⬥

When he entered the Cat's Tail Gambling Pit, Jonny was frisked by two henchmen. "Be careful where you grab, Mikey," Jonny said as dedicated hands ran up and down his body. Mikey grunted, then turned to his brother guarding the Pit's entrance. "He's clean."

Despite being a sunny day outside, the inside was gloomy with the only light being a scatter of orange lights just bright enough for customers to see the cards and the dancing girls.

Jonny was quickly escorted toward a round table in a back room. Over deafening music and even louder shouts, laughs, cursing, and threats, he heard Greco's shrill voice even before he saw him. When he did see the bushy-haired Greek, he had a half-dressed girl sitting on his lap. Four other men were glaring at their cards.

"Raise yeah a hundred," Greco shouted as he pulled away from the lips of the young girl. One man folded, another called his raise, while the third and the fourth had not yet made up their minds. Soon the third shook his head and threw his cards on the table, leaving only Greco and the fourth man.

Greco took a quick look at his cards and smiled. "Come on Harlow, shit or get off the pot."

Looking over Greco's shoulder and that of his heavily tattooed girlfriend, Jonny could now see his hand: a lonely Queen of hearts and four other non-royal cards. He was bluffing. Jonny shook his head, *Jesus, no wonder the jerk is so far in debt.*

Finally, Greco's raise was called and raised again by the remaining man. Knowing his bluff failed, Greco muttered a curse then turned to Jonny as he slammed his cards down and headed towards the bar. He gave Jonny a frustrated look as he sat down. "Damn it, Jonny B, you brought me a shit of bad luck. What are doing here anyway?"

Before Jonny could answer, Greco shouted to the dark-haired, robust waitress. "Another beer!"

"One for me, too," Jonny said. "Just happened to be in the area, and thought I might drop by and see how you're doing."

"Don't play with me, Jonny, I know--"

"No games, Nicky, just a friendly conversation, but, the boss did ask me to remind you about the money you owe him if I got a chance to see you."

"Yea! I thought there was something on your mind or Vallario's mind. Just tell him I--"

"I'm afraid you will have to tell him."

Pounding pulse, eyes wide open, Greco turned pale. "Can't you tell him you couldn't find me? Do that and I'll go away! Just disappear!"

Jonny put his arm on Greco's shaking arm and shook his head. "Nicky, I don't care about how much you owe or who you owe it to, but the boss does. You can't walk away from this, so I suggest you discuss the issue with him. He *suggested* you see him by tomorrow."

"Look, I know I'm overdue with the money, but I've had a lot of bad luck with the cards recently, and I got a busy schedule. You know, dealing with the sharks and all."

"This is not me asking. It's the boss who's asking. I'm just the middle man, someone who tries to mediate disputes to avoid violence when possible. So I suggest you reschedule your schedule and see Mister Vallario tomorrow . . . about three o'clock. He can be very impatient at times." It did not take a genius for Nicky to understand the message.

After Jonny left, Nicky went to the bathroom and flooded his face with cold water. He was in a dilemma. Could he convince Vallario that he could still come up with the sixty large he *borrowed* from the *Company?* That would give him some time to dodge the sharks who wanted the thousands owed to them. Knowing that not doing both would be fatal, he started crying. "What the hell," he mumbled.

He tried to comfort himself with the thought that sending Jonny with the message was a good sign. "Shit," he whispered as he looked in the bathroom mirror. "If Vallario wasn't willing to give me more time, he wouldn't have sent someone else instead of the wimp he did send. Hell!" he grunted as he dried his face. "Vallario will wait a few more days."

Eight o'clock. Saturday evening, Alonzo Vallario looked at his watch. Then he made a phone call. "Durand, I think it's time to use the stick."

Durand laughed. "Yea, the *stick*. I'm on it, Boss."

⬖ ◆ ◆ ⬗

Greco was not the first person who got *the stick*. It started with a stream of bad events a few years after he made his way up the Mafia ladder to being a Don. His wife left him when his son, Nicolo, was young. Although the boy stayed with his father, thanks to a friendly court judge, his wife was dead to him. Being used to having control of his life and that of others, he felt helpless for the first time. All he had left was his power as a Don and a spoiled son.

He made it clear to everyone that power was more important to him than anything else. Although his son had the best schools, the best tutors, the best of everything, Vallario's neglect overshadowed everything and everybody. The boy took advantage of this. Being the son of a powerful man, made him believe he was also powerful. He got away with things, things that would put others in jail or worse. In fact, Nicolo did do time in the big house. Just before he was eligible for parole someone put a shiv in his back. Although he survived, Vallario always thought it was one of the Irish that had tried to kill him.

Once out of prison, Nicole became even wilder. Addicted to gambling, he was at someone's table every night. Worse, he liked to play with the Irish gangs. Since he was a dependent loser, the Irish welcomed him. That didn't concern him; there was always money available for a Don's son. One day he went to play but never came back. The next day he was found floating in the river. That tore Vallario up. It was then he realized that being a Don's son did not necessarily make it safe in his father's line of business. So he sent Nicolo's two young sons to live with their grandmother in California.

Although the Irish and the Italian mobs were often at war with each other, the loss of his son made Vallario their worst enemy. He always looked for a chance to take revenge, and this was a good reason. Believing his driver had failed to protect his son, he sent him instead of one of his hitmen to fix things, to the extent things could be fixed.

Jonny was working late the night the driver was to go after the Irish. He figured he would need a driver if he was to going to do the shooting, so he put Jonny behind the wheel. That was the first time Jonny was involved in anything more than tampering with the books. Shaking nervously, Jonny parked in front of the building where the Irish played while the driver went into the room with a sawed-off shotgun. Three minutes and two gunshots later, he pushed Jonny onto the passenger's side, got behind the wheel, and drove away.

Although Jonny was not the shooter, he felt he was just as guilty for four Irish men scattered over the floor. It would take him a long time to get over it . . . if he ever would. Two weeks later, the driver disappeared and was replaced.

CHAPTER 2

Lieutenant Kaminski was on the phone when Detective Janson knocked on his door. Kaminski covered the phone with his hand and gave a sharp, "Come in."

"Yankee, the body we found was--"

Kaminski cut him off with a sharp hand in the air, then went back to his phone call. After a few minutes and several *uh-huhs*, he put the phone down. Janson tried to finish his report. "It's about the body we found, we ID'd him."

Again he was stopped by the Lieutenant. "A phone call was ahead of you, Detective. His name was Greco, James Greco, AKA Nicky The Greek."

Janson narrowed his brows in confusion. "Jesus Christ, Lieutenant, I just found out about it. How did you know so soon?"

"That's why you're a Detective, Janson, and I'm a Lieutenant." After a minute of thought, the grey-haired Lieutenant continued. "He's . . . or was connected with the Vallario organization. We had him in court for various things at one time or another, drugs, loan sharking, gambling. You name it, and his fingers prints were all over it. But thanks to expensive lawyers and last-minute missing witnesses, nothing would stick. The good news for us, if there is any, is we don't have to deal with him any longer. Since most of his stuff was federal, we'll shove him over to the FBI's Organization Crime Office."

Janson shrugged his shoulders. "That was my thinking, too. I'll contact Agents Ryan and Finch and let them know they have it."

"Let'em know we'll help on this end if help is needed. While we're waiting for the feds to get involved, you hit the streets and see if you can get any clues to who might have done the city the favor of putting one of Vallario's pets to bed."

�⊷ ❖ ⊶桊⊷

Jonny had just got off the phone with his Mexican contacts embedded in the city when the phone rang again. It was Linny Calabrese. "Jonny, Mister V wanted me to let you know about last night's *incident*."

"Incident?"

"Yeah. The incident he called a *four-flusher versus the sharks*."

"You've lost me, Linny."

"I guess he didn't take your visit seriously. Anyway, someone else visited him late last night. Vallario thinks it was one of the sharks."

"Do you believe that?"

"Jonny, I get paid to believe everything I'm told. I suggest you do the same thing. But I'm just sayin' whoever

13

it was resolved the Greeks problems. So now, he's in *retirement*."

After a deep breath, Jonny continued. "Well, I made it clear to him he had to come up with the money he owed. Everybody in this business should know there are no retirement benefits."

After hanging up the phone, Jonny banged his fist on his desk and shook his head. "I knew if he did not show up on time with or without the money, something bad was going to happen." He banged his desk again and shook his head. "I might not have pulled the trigger, but I was part of the murder . . . again! I should have warned him of the consequences if he . . ." Even as he blamed himself, he knew once he delivered the *message*, he had no further control.

He considered leaving the *Company*, but he knew he couldn't . . . he knew much, saw too much, did too much. There was only one way of quitting the *Company*. Still, the thought dwelled in his mind. *Maybe someday, somehow, I can make a real negotiation with Vallario.*

❖ ❖

It always began pleasantly enough – sunny beaches, barefoot in the sand, palm trees waving to the rhythm of a gentle wind. Then he was on a yacht with the wind moving him towards a small island. He was content–no problems, no phone calls, no negotiations. Suddenly, the wind turns against him, blue skies became thunderstorm-dark with waves crashing over the sides of the squeaking boat. Then Jonny woke from his nightly dream . . . a dream that always turned into a nightmare.

His sweating face buried in shaking hands, he tried to push the nightmare out of his head. Slowly, reality returned. As usual, he realized the dream was just vain hopes and wishes – the nightmare part was reality.

After a hot shower and a shot of bourbon, he picked out a suit and tie–his daily disguise. After dressing, there was the daily knock on the door. "Okay, I'll be there in a minute," he shouted. Grabbing his overcoat, he opened the door. He expected to see his driver, Joe Leone. Transportation in a limousine was one of the perks of being employed by a mobster. To his surprise, it wasn't the driver. Instead, he was greeted with a man and a woman, each flashing a badge.

"Good morning, Mister Milano," the red-haired woman said. "I'm Ann Ryan. This is my partner, Jacob Finch. We would like to ask you a few questions about--"

"I'm sorry, but you caught me on my way to work. Perhaps you--"

"Yes, I know," the man said. "Since you work for Alonzo Vallario, we thought it might be more comfortable if we talked to you here . . . you do work for Alonzo Vallario, don't you?"

"Yes . . . I'm his accountant, but--"

"Can we come in?" Agent Ryan interrupted. "We won't take much of your time. However, if you prefer, we can go downtown and have our discussion."

Jonny took a deep breath. "No! That won't be necessary," Jonny said as he backed away from the door.

Once inside, Agent Ryan looked around the living room. "Nice home you have here, Mister Milano. Didn't know accountants made this much money."

"I do okay," Jonny said as he pointed to two leather chairs. "Make yourself comfortable."

Finch sat down on one of the chairs while Ryan ran her hand over the soft leather but remained standing. A *Power play*. Jonny had seen it before. He let it pass then went back to wondering why two FBI agents were interested enough about him that they would be in his living room, especially so early in the morning. "Now, just what can I do for the FBI?"

Finch looked up at Jonny who was still standing next to his partner. "We're not sure, Mister Milano, but--"

"If you're not sure then maybe you need to come back when--"

Ryan cut him off. Jonny just smiled. *Another power play*. "What Agent Finch means, Mister Milano, is if you know a man named Nickolas Greco?" When Jonny didn't answer, she continued. "He also goes by the nickname, Nicky The Greek."

Jonny narrowed his eyes then, "Yes, I know him. Mister Greco works for Mister Vallario. Why do you ask?"

"Mister Greco was found dead in his apartment this morning," Agent Ryan said.

"Dead!" Jonny said with a wrinkled brow as if he didn't already know what was coming. "I just saw him yesterday in the elevator. I heard he had a heart condition, but he looked okay then."

"It wasn't his heart," Finch said. "He was murdered."

Jonny grunted and shook his head. "I'm sorry to hear about him dying . . . but being murdered! You think it was a robbery? After all, he did live in a pretty bad neighborhood."

"You seem to know more about him than you think," Ryan said. "But this wasn't a robbery. Nothing was taken."

After a brief pause and searching the Agent's faces, Jonny sat down on the leather couch. "I only know what I hear. However, I do know that local murders and crimes are usually handled by the police. Why is the FBI involved?"

Agent Ryan looked at her partner then at Jonny. "You seem to know about the law also."

"Not a lot, but I know when the FBI gets involved it's not a local issue. So why is the FBI involved?"

"The NYPD knew Greco worked for your boss, Alonzo Vallario, someone the FBI has had its eyes on for a long time. They realized they had their hands full, so they called us in to bail them out. But we were already ahead of them."

"Ahead of them?"

"Yes. We've had Vallario and *all his employees* on our list of people of interest for a long time," Ryan said with a smirk.

Jonny smiled and ignored the emphasis the agent put on *all his employees*. "And since when did employment become a crime, Agent?"

Ryan's smirk turned into a wide smile. "Of course it's not a crime, Mister Milano, but it can still be an item of interest."

"Agent Ryan is right, Mister Milano, but the way he was killed, a bullet in the back of his head, has a strong Mob smell, especially when you look at everything Greco was believed to be involved in . . . extortion, drug trafficking, loan sharking . . . and probably other things we don't know about."

The agent's exchange of looks made it clear to Jonny that they were trying to pull a truck with a bicycle. "So you have evidence that Mister Greco was involved in all of these *crimes?*"

"A list of charges," Finch said as he looked at Agent Ryan, "but no evidence that was strong to hold up in court."

"This is America, Agent. Charges are not the same as guilt . . . unless you have evidence."

"Good point, Mister Milano," Ryan added with a grin. "But what we consider strong evidence isn't always strong enough for some judges. That's also something that concerns us. Anyway, when the locals decided they had more than they could handle, you know, with Greco's history and all, they passed the ball. So we're bailing them out again."

"With due respect, Agent, I have my own problems. So tell me, why do I have two FBI agents in my house questioning me about a man I know little about? A man I may have or may not have said hello to on the company elevator at one time or another."

"Mister Milano, I assure you, we're questioning *everyone* who had contact with James Greco, not just you," Agent Ryan said in an irritated tone. "However, I find it strange that no one seems to know him and his off-work activities."

"I can assure you, Miss Ryan, I don't know what Mister Greco was or was not doing on his off time."

"It's Agent Ryan! And I'm sorry to make you late for work, but--"

Being aware of his partner's quick temper when challenged or addressed as a female rather than an FBI agent, Agent Finch interrupted her. "I think we're done here." Then handed Jonny a card. "If you think of anything that would help us, you can contact us here." Then the two agents left.

While he was waiting for his ride to Vallario Inc., Jonny decided he needed to find out who else the feds had visited and what they might have said. He had the nagging feeling that he might become the dupe if Greco's murder could be linked to his boss. He had seen it done before. Minutes later, Vallario's driver, Leone, picked him up in the company's SUV. Both were quiet during the twenty-minute drive to work, but when they moved into the underground parking lot, Leone looked at Jonny through the rearview mirror. "Looked like you had company, Jonny. Anyone I know?"

"Just a couple of friends from the FBI. But I think you already know that."

"And what did you tell them?" Leone asked.

"I told them my name, but they already knew it. I told them I knew Greco. They knew that, too. I also told them we were not close."

"The Greek's departure upset me," Leone said. "I liked the man."

"Did the boss--"

Leone cut Jonny off with a glare easily seen in the rearview mirror. "Jonny, you're his accountant . . . you handle the financial side of his operation, so let me give you some advice, my friend, what the boss knows or doesn't know, or what he has done or not done, is over your paygrade."

"Thanks, for the clarification. However, finding the FBI at my doorstep investing a murder of one of our employees troubles me."

Leone opened the back door, handed Jonny his attaché case then patted him on his back. "Jonny, I know it's distressful when you try to make the unbalanced books balance. But things the feds see as being across the line are just part of the *business* . . . part of the job. Shit, man! Every company does it at one time or another."

"Was killing Greco part of the job?"

Leone stepped closer to Jonny, looked around then whispered, "Be careful where you tread, Jonny. Greco betrayed the boss's trust when he took money from the *Business* to pay his drug and gambling bills. Hell, he even owed me a lot of money as well as the loan sharks! It was just a matter of time before someone made him pay the piper. The boss had me talk to the sharks Greco owed. Know what they told me? *Tough Shit!* I wanted the boss to take sixty-thousand out of their asses, but he didn't want to start a war, so I asked him if he wanted me to take it out of the Greco's ass. He said he preferred to handle it more civilly . . . if possible. That's what the boss said."

"And what did he mean, *more civilly?*" Jonny asked with a smirk.

"There's a lot of civil ways, Jonny, but I think the Greek owed the sharks a lot more than sixty grand, and they're not as forgiving as the boss. But how the feds focused on you is still a mystery to me. It's best to just let it ride and be careful, Jonny B. Eventually, the feds will find someone else to haunt." After a long pause, he muttered, "Jonny, I learned from the boss there are two ways to get things done . . . the *carrot* or the *stick*. Vallario usually prefers the stick . . . that's how I got my job."

After going to his office, Jonny tossed his attache onto the desk and checked his phone messages. The first two were complaints of petty issues. The third was from Vallario. The call wasn't unusual, but the tone was. When he entered Vallario's office, his tall, long-legged secretary was painting her nails. He tapped on her desk to get her attention. "Kelly, the boss left me a message saying he wanted to see me."

She responded with a seductive smile. "He's on the phone, blue eyes, but I'll tell him you're here."

When Jonny entered his office, Vallario was hanging up his phone. "I was just talking with my PD contact. He called as soon as he heard about the Greek. He tried to convince his superiors that Greco's departure was something they should handle, but the son-a-bitches punted and passed it on to the feds." Pointing to a chair, he continued. "What concerns me more, however, is having two fed agents questioning you."

"News travel's fast, Boss. Badges flashing at me so early in the morning troubles me, too."

"I want to hear what they had to say."

"They asked if I knew Nicky . . . were we close . . . what was his job here at the company . . . did he have any obvious enemies."

"Jonny, you're my accountant and a damn good one at that, but I hope you didn't tell them that Greco was taking money from the *Business* . . . my money, to pay his drug and gambling bills."

"Of course not. I just gave them routine answers to routine questions."

"Good. Knowing he was ripping off the company would raise their eyebrows. Early today, I called the loan sharks he owed. Know what they told me . . . me, a Don? *Tough Shit! He still owes us twenty large.* I was so pissed off that I thought about taking the money, *my money,* Greco paid them out of their asses. Other Dons pressed me to take it out of the Greek's ass, but his ass wasn't worth anything close to the dough he chiseled out of the Company. But killing him over sixty grand? I don't think so! But the sharks ain't that forgiving. When they realized he wasn't going to pay, they got tired of his excuses and threats . . . well, you know the results of that."

"Mister Vallario, protecting your money is my job. However, when our . . . *your* contacts can't keep this issue in the house, and I'm the first to be questioned by the FBI, I get a little jittery."

"I don't know why they focused on you, but don't worry. I take care of my people. Besides, they're like vultures, they'll peck at decaying meat on the road then fly off to find something more decaying. Anyway, you shouldn't get any more FBI visitors. But it would help me if you, *as a concerned consultant*, could let the NYPD know about Greco's gambling debts. If they pass it on to the feds, it might take the spotlight off the *Office*; the *Office* you are part of." After lighting a Cuban cigar, he pointed his finger at Jonny. "After that, it might be a good idea for you to take a vacation, at least until the vultures find other meat."

Vallario seemed nervous. Jonny understood wanting the feds to know about Greco's gambling debts. That would take their focus off the company and give them another path to follow. He even understood not wanting them to know about the money he stole from the Company. That would only put more focus on the *Company*. What he did not understand, however, was Vallario wanting him to go away. That troubled him, but he tried not to show it as he nodded. "You're right, boss. A few days away might just be what I need." He started to leave then turned around. "Before I leave, there's another issue we need to discuss . . . college for your grandkids."

Vallario sighed then shook his head. "Where does time go, Jonny? Yesterday they were bouncing on my lap; today going to college. Now I don't even get to see them."

"They're a bit wild, but considering not having a father anymore, and a mother so far away, they've turned out pretty good. But it might be best for them . . . you know, not being around the *Company*."

It was the first time anyone saw Alonzo Vallario with tears in his eyes. "Set up a fund, but you control it. I don't want her to get a penny of it."

As soon as Jonny left the office, Vallario called Linny Calabrese into his office. "Linny," he said in a soft tone, "you're pretty close to Jonny, aren't you?"

Linny nodded. "Yeah, I'd say so. Jonny and I go way back."

"Well, I'm a little worried about him," Vallario said, again his voice was lowered. "He does a good job of handling the flow of money in and out of our company without questions and uses his knowledge of forensic accounting to change any questionable issue to our advantage, but his meeting with Greco didn't go well."

"That's unusual for Jonny. Couldn't he find him?"

"He found him all right. Gave him an option to make things right, but the horse thief didn't take him seriously and continued throwing away more money. Guess the Greek forgot there were other ways to deal with horse thieves."

Laughing, Linny said, "In the old west, they just hanged 'em."

Showing a hint of a smile, something he rarely shared, Vallario, looked at Linny, "As Clint said, *hang 'em high*. The smile quickly faded as he patted the ash from his cigar into an ashtray. Then he continued, now in a more disturbing tone. "What happened to the Greek doesn't bother me. What does bother me is *Mister Milano*. If our friends in the NYPD fail to keep the feds at bay and they press him, he might panic and change *his* loyalty."

"Jonny? I don't think so, Boss. But if you want, I'll push the vacation issue, and suggest he goes somewhere down south for a while."

"Good. Keeping him away from this whole mess is a good idea for *everybody*."

CHAPTER 3

Jonny was deep in *fixing* recent *financials* when his phone rang. It was Linny. "A vacation? Christ, Linny, I'm up to my neck with crap I need to do and you want me to take time off.

"Jonny, there's a lot more things in life than tampering books for . . . for someone. Besides, that *someone* thinks you've been working too hard, that's all."

"*Working hard* is my job, Linny. Besides, where in the hell would I go if I did take one?"

"There's a lot more places to go than this hellhole."

"And what about the Mexicans and their gouging prices?"

"The boss says you can negotiate with them while you're away. If not, they can wait." His voice now lowered, he continued. "Listen, Jonny, Vallario wants you gone for a while. With the feds putting their nose in Nicky's murder, he thinks someone might turn him over."

"Who would be that stupid?"

"Jonny, you are high on that list. I assured him you could be trusted, but with the feds' sudden interest in you . . . well he's a bit paranoid."

"Paranoid? I don't know why. He's got dozens of men looking over his back for him. Anyway, you might be right. Getting out of the city until the Greco issue fades might be in my best interest, too. Other than Company business, I haven't been anywhere in the past few years. Linny, I wouldn't even know where to go."

"Christ, Jonny. Go where everyone goes on vacations, the beach."

"The beach? I . . . I don't know, Linny. Other than dreams about walking on one, I've never actually been to one."

After a deep breath, Linny laughed. "I should have such dreams, Jonny B. All mine are about . . . well, they're not wasted on beaches. But go with your dreams. Let them take you out of NYC and see the rest of the world. There's a lot of good beaches down south. All you have to do is pick one."

"No. Not that far away from the city."

"Damn it, Jonny. Forget about the city for a couple of weeks. That's what vacations are for."

"I want to be a car--drive back to the city if I'm needed."

"Jonny Blue, you are one stubborn son of a bitch. Okay, go to Sag Island. Although it's not as far away as I think you should go, it might be far enough to keep you out of the spotlight until the Greek issue fades."

The next morning Jonny packed a suitcase, put a hold on his mail, and left on his *vacation*. During his drive to

Sag Island, he realized he would have to leave the *Business* someday. Not only would it be an easy decision, it could also be a fatal one. One unanswered question began to flow through his mind. *Did Vallario order Greco's murder, or was it on the loan sharks?* Although one was as likely as the other, he chose to believe that the sharks were the culprits. Whichever it was, Greco would not be missed by anyone; not the Vallario family, the Basilone family, the Civiciro family, or the Moretti families . . . or by the Sharks.

I didn't like the man, Jonny said to himself, *but it's sad for anyone to die and not have someone to miss you.* Then a contemptuous laugh, followed by a deep breath. *The truth, at least in the eyes of the Mafia, is we are all potential remnants living on borrowed time. The only question is, who will be next?*

The further he got out of the Big City and its noise, traffic, and skyscrapers, the more he felt he was leaving a part of his life behind him. Miles later, as Sag Island got closer, the soft wind, fresh air, and silence brought him another feeling, one he had not felt in a long time . . . freedom.

It didn't take much time to reach Sag Island and less time to find a small beach house. "Kitchen and all. Not bad . . . if you can cook," he said to himself as he glanced over the two rooms. After cleaning up, he poked the bed's mattress then flopped on it. As he gazed at the pop-corn ceiling, he realized freedom wasn't as easy as he thought it would be. He tried to put the FBI, the Mafia, and Greco out of his mind.

His first walk on the sand in a gentle breeze with seagulls dipping into realms of water that gradually turned into blistering waves that crashed onto the beach only to gently drift back, made him realize the city he left was just a *place*, and he just a servant to the demands of others. Here he felt he could be a freeman. "But freedom comes with a price," he told himself. "Maybe, by finishing the unfinished, leaving will be easier."

While nights were sleepless, days strolling on the soft sand with foaming seawater breaking over his feet, let him slowly fight back the building rage over things he could not control: The Mexican problem, who killed Nicky the Greek, why he was suddenly sent away. Finally, the suffocating troubles of the past began to be replaced with thoughts of a future in a less violent world free of anxiety that gradually turns into fear. Only if he left the Company could he enter this world.

Once back at the beach house, he made contact with the Mexicans. Carlo Garcia's middleman answered the phone . . . Garcia's phone, the phone he always answered himself. After minutes listening to excuses, Jonny interrupted him. "Tell Senor Garcia that Jonny Milano wants to talk to him."

A long pause then, "I'll see if he's here."

"See if he's here? If he wasn't there you wouldn't be there."

"I said I would see if he's here!" Other than murmuring in the background, the phone was quiet. Finally, the man was back on the phone. "Senor Garcia is not here."

"When Senor Garcia *comes back*, tell him Don Vallario won't be happy with his excuses, much less being ignored. That's something Senor Garcia should think about." After minutes of quietness other than more background mutters, the phone went dead. Then he called Vallario.

"Mister Vallario, I don't know what Garcia is up to, but the son of a bitch wouldn't talk to me. I would take that response as a *no response*."

Vallario wasn't happy with the news. "They're asking for trouble."

"I can try to contact him again, but--"

"Forget about him . . . for now. But I promise you, things will get better after my next *offer*."

Jonny shook his head after hanging up. Vallario's tone told him the next offer from him would only make things worse. Another lesson learned . . . trying to finish the unfinishable was not always possible. Days later he learned another lesson, walking barefoot on the beach made sore feet and tired legs. Nights at the local bar eased these but did little to ease his frustration. Then he met someone at Tuckers Tavern who pushed the FBI, Vallario, Greco, and the Mexican Cartel out of his mind. She was a petite, 24-year-old waitress with a strong southern drawl and soft brown skin that complemented her Latina name, Carlene Sabella.

Over the past few years, Carlene had moved from one city to another, one waitress job to another, until she ended up at Havens Beach and Tucker's Tavern. When she met Jonny, she saw something about him that eased her sullied opinion of men. Her talent of showing friendliness while avoiding the smirch of flirtation impressed Jonny. After several nights at the tavern, throwing quarters into the jukebox playing songs he never listened to and ordering food he never ate, he asked her if she would have a drink with him after her shift. She gently turned him down.

"I'm sorry, Mister Milano, but it's against the bar's rule to hang around after the shift. Anyway, my shift ends when the bar closes."

"You might as well jerk off, old man," a slurred voice shouted from the end of the bar. "The bitch tinks sheee's better than her customers!"

"You need to watch your language, fella," Jonny said as he glared at the drunk.

"Don't pay any attention to Butch," Carlene said with a shake of her head. "He always has a filthy mouth."

When Carlene ignored him, Butch staggered over to Jonny's table. "Hey! You deaf?" the drunk shouted again. "Get your ass up and get me another drink!"

Jonny got up from the table and looked face-to-face with Butch. "For the last time, show the lady some respect or get out of here!"

The drunk laughed. "You and who else gonna make me leave?"

Jonny looked at Carlene. "Excuse me for a minute." Before she could answer, he grabbed the drunk by his collar and dragged him across the room, opened the door with one hand, and tossed him out with the other.

"Wow, I didn't see that coming," Carlene said when Jonny sat back down.

Jonny responded with a half-grin. "I don't think he did either."

Suddenly the door opened then slammed shut. Butch was back in the bar. "Yous tank you can treat Butch Harlow dat way and get away wit it?" he grumbled as he pointed a swaying Glock at Jonny's face. "I'm gonna--" Before Butch could finish his threat, Jonny waved one hand across the man's chest and grabbed the gun with the other hand. Butch's wide-opened eyes showed his shock over the speed that took away his advantage.

While Butch was still stunned, Jonny dropped the gun's clip to the floor then jerked back the slide sending the last bullet in the gun over his head. Then he handed Butch the empty gun. "Make sure you're not drunk the next time you point this at someone. Now go home while you can and sober up." Without saying another word, Butch stumbled out of the bar.

Carlene shook her head in surprise. "Where did you learn that little trick?"

"I watch a lot of movies," Jonny said with another half-grin, then sat back down next to the surprised woman. "What I was about to say before this interruption was, do you like the beach?"

Carlene raised an eyebrow and nodded. "Sure. No need to be so close to one and not go there."

They met on the beach several days over the next week. Mostly small talk on his part, the story of her life on her part.

"I was born and raised in a small town in Clayton, Georgia. And I mean *small*. After graduating from high school, I planned on going to college and getting a Social Worker degree, but that didn't work out. Who knows, maybe I'll do still do that . . . one day."

"What stopped you in the first place, love or money?" Jonny asked.

"A bit of both. I was only eighteen and just out of high school when my parents were killed in an auto accident. With them gone, I was pretty much alone. I had no money and no experience on how to get any. That changed when I met someone at the bar where I worked . . . so I thought. Anyway, poor naive me, it was love at first sight. As far as love on his part, if there was any, he shared it with most of the girls in our small town."

"We all make mistakes," Jonny said. "I've sure made my share. But sometimes we belittle ourselves over things we have no control over. So I'd be careful before I would assume anything was a *mistake*."

"I guess you're right, we do have control to some extent." A deep breath followed. "Is marrying someone you love or just living with them after a year of drug, alcohol, and abuse a mistake?"

"I don't know, Carlene. Sometimes it's difficult to know what is *just life* and what is a mistake."

Carlene was quiet for a minute then shook her head. "Fate or mistake, does it really matter? The outcome is the same."

"You got me there. Either way, many outcomes are repairable, at least to some extent. Just like you corrected the *mistake* after you saw what that *someone* was like and left him."

"I can't take credit for correcting anything. If my husband hadn't been found dead in his car, I might still be with him. Good or bad, I was left alone again with only twenty-thousand dollars from his life insurance. There was little left for college after paying off his debts." What she did not tell Jonny was, although the police didn't think twenty-thousand dollars was enough of a motive to kill anyone, a year of physical and psychological abuse might be.

"So how did you end up here in another small town?"

"I had to settle down somewhere. Here was better than most of the towns I had been in. Anyway, that's my story. How about yours?"

"Other than going to college with plans to get a business degree that didn't work out, there's nothing much to tell."

"So, John Milano came into the world as an adult?"

"Not quite, and Jonny is my real name, not a nickname."

"Sounds like there's a story somewhere there," Carlene said with an accusing glare.

"Humm, I guess you could call it a story. Whatever you call it, it was sorta weird. It began with a quarrel between my mother and father. Mom wanted a girl and was going to name her Joann. Dad wanted a boy and wanted to name him John. Dad got his son, but he had to negotiate over the name. In the end, they agreed on Jonny."

"I must admit that is a weird story."

Jonny smiled. "I told you it was. The worse part was going through life being called *Jonny Boy*. Later, Jonny Boy turned into *Jonny Blue Eyes* . . . you know, blue eyes on an

Italian. It didn't take long for everyone to shorten Jonny Blue Eyes to Jonny B."

Carlene laughed. "Those blue eyes just begged a nickname." Then she took a small camera from her purse and pointed it at Jonny. "Smile, Jonny B, the camera is watching."

"No, no, no," Jonny said as he tried to move away. "I hate pictures of me."

"Well, we'll have to hate them together." After a few clicks, she moved closer. "I believe this is what they call a *selfie*." Click, click again.

Carlene made Jonny feel alive. Something he had not felt in a long time; something he could not quite put his finger on. Whatever it was made him want to stay at Havens Beach.

Being twenty years older than her, he was quick to rule out a romantic relationship. For most men, that would not be an obstacle, but he had seen too many men taking advantage of younger girls then dumping them. Despite his questionable integrity, he had boundaries he would not cross. Taking advantage of the innocent was one of them. Besides, his time was limited.

Jonny spent his nights worrying about his company and the Cartel and his days walking in the sand with Carlene. However, he kept in touch with Linny. On his last call, he learned that the Cartels had backed down on increasing the merchandise prices. That gave him hope that the unfixable had finally been fixed. It didn't take long for hope to fade; the Cartels reneged on their agreement. One or two things would have to happen, let the cocaine, heroin, and meth business dry up or buy drugs at a higher price. One way or another, he no longer cared.

⟞⟜ ❖ ❖ ⟜⟝

A week after arriving at Havens beach, Jonny packed his bag to return to the city. On his way out, he stopped by Tucker's Tavern to tell Carlene goodbye. She wasn't there. Part of him was glad she wasn't. It made leaving a bit easier than saying goodbye in person, while another part drowned in disappointment.

"She left you a *See You Again* note," Tucker said as he reached under the counter. "Oh, yea, she left a phone number too, and this."

"That's a picture she took of us on the beach."

"Here, take it. She liked it so much she gave me one, too."

CHAPTER 4

It had been four months since Jonny left Havens Beach – four months without calling Carlene. He picked up his phone like he did every day, but like every day, he never dialed her. Thoughts of her faded as he focused on the Cartel and its failure to live up to the verbal contract they agreed to.

Drugs from Mexico were slowing. This put a drain on Mafia income. Concerns and apprehension were building. Vallario believed war with the Cartels was unavoidable. While the Alonzo Vallario Company was large enough and powerful enough to have its way in New York and a few of the surrounding states, a war south of the border was far more than he alone could win. Only if all of the Mafia families agreed, could they put enough pressure on the Mexican drug lords to get them to give in and reduce their prices.

It wasn't long before Vallario told Jonny to schedule a meeting with the other Dons. Other than Don Angelo De Luca, everyone agreed a meeting was due, but he decided to attend when he realized he would be shut out and not have a voice in the group's discussion. The meeting, boasting six-thousand-dollar Weller Kentucky bourbon and even more expensive Musigny Grand wine, along with a dozen affable waitresses, was going well. . . that was until Vallario hit the Dons with a bombshell. "Why are we even discussing this? The bastards will squeeze us until we hurt so much that we will come crawling to them. This Don, Don Vallario, will go it alone before he yields any more ground."

De Luca stood up, hammered his fist on the table, and glared at Vallario. "Alonzo is a war hawk. Don't listen to his nonsense. His plan will hurt our profits even more."

The room was suddenly quiet until Vallario stood up. "Yes, De Luca is right. It will hurt us more, but we have other options to make up for the losses, they do not. Once they see we are together, they will be crawling to us." Whispers around the room as each Don discussed things with another Don.

Realizing this was an opportunity to hit De Luca with a final arrow, Vallario raised his hand for silence. "My friend, Don De Luca, always sees the downside of a problem. He would rather go the easy way, the foolish way, of doing nothing." Looking now directly at De Luca, he continued. "But I tell you, doing nothing is the worst thing we can do!"

"Ask yourself why would Vallario draw us into a war . . . a war we would lose. Ask what he would gain."

Don Marco Civiciro stood up in support of Vallario. "Alonzo is right. Doing nothing will only make things worse." Then he turned to De Luca. "Being obsessive might be okay with those blonde tarts Angelo chases, but it's not okay with business decisions. I cannot join him in his obsession that the Mexican solution is *doing nothing!*"

Don Moretti laughed then tried to temper the atmosphere. "Marco, what would life be without blonde tarts?" Everyone laughed, including De Luca. "But, we must be realistic. Alonzo has a strong point. Higher prices or war seem to be the only options. We must choose."

Hiding his anger behind a shield of laughter, De Luca sat back down and gulped down a glass of wine. "If we could take out some of the Mexican Cartels without an uproar on both sides of the border, then I would consider a war, but--"

"Angelo, my friend, we all hear you," Vallario said in an empathetic tone. "But we have to do something."

De Luca again, but in a more somber tone. "So you would sacrifice what we do have by--"

Before De Luca could finish his words, Vallario cut him off. "If you watch any movies, my friend, you should know that Ninjas can be more productive than any army."

"Movies are not reality, Alonzo."

"You are right again . . . to some extent," Vallario said. "But I know this to be a reality: unless we get Garcia's Los Zetas's Cartel's attention, we will soon be the puppets and they will be the puppeteers. I can't. . .I won't let that happen!" After letting his words sink in, he continued. "Is anyone else against this?" When no one answered, he looked at De Luca again. "It's decision time, my friend. You're either with us or you're not."

Now angered at the dominance Vallario had over the Dons, De Luca looked around the table. "You know this man. He would send a hundred men with AKAs over the border if he had them."

"Gentlemen, Angelo speaks the truth," Vallario said. "If I had an army, I would send it over the border with AKAs and tanks, if I had them, but I don't have them, and we won't need them. There is another fact in our favor. Some of my southern sources in the Sinaloa Cartel agree there needs to some leadership changes on their side of the border."

Vallario made eye-contact with each Don. De Luca started to speak again, but seeing he was the only one in disagreement, he just folded his arms and gave Vallario a surly look, making it clear he was not persuaded. Vallario ignored him and stood up again. "Then we all agree to resolve this problem on our terms. There will still be resistance down south, but eventually, they will come around."

❖ ❖

It was raining when Jonny, Sonny Fazio, Francis Mancini, Joe Ricco, and Linny Calabrese's plane landed at Ciudad Juarez airport. After picking up their carry-on bags, Mancini gave Jonny a scorning look. "Since you know these jerks, *Mister Businessman*, you make the call."

"That's all I'm going to do, Francis. I'm not going to be involved beyond that!"

"Yeah, we know," Fazio said with a smirk. "You're just the *negotiator*."

Jonny ignored him and headed towards a pay phone and dialed a number. "This is Jonny Milano. Let me speak to Senor Garcia . . . Yes, he's expecting me."

Garcia was quick to answer the phone. "I was waiting for your call, Senor Milano."

After several minutes, Jonny hung up and turned to the four men. "I thought he would want to meet somewhere quiet, so I suggested our hotel room. But he's a suspicious man."

Fazio grumbled, "What the . . . We're the ones that should be suspicious."

"He wants to meet me at the Maria Chuchena Restaurant at seven-thirty . . . and he emphasized *only me*."

Fazio interrupted him with an arrogant sneer and said, "Then why the hell did we have to come?"

"You're here because your boss wanted you to be here, Fazio," Jonny said with an impatient tone. "I can't tell you more than that because I don't know more than that. But since you are here you might as well fill up on some real Mexican cuisine."

"Hell, Fazio, You might even get lucky," Linny said as he punched him on the arm. "There's bound to be a blind girl around somewhere."

While everyone but Fazio was laughing, Jonny flagged down a cab and they headed to the center of Juarez. During the ride, Mancini whispered to Jonny, "There could be a lot of people there."

Jonny shrugged his shoulders. "I doubt he'll want to discuss Cartel business in a crowded restaurant. Since he doesn't want the hotel room, he'll probably want to use the conference room. But it doesn't matter to me; his territory, his rules. Wherever he wants, I go alone or he'll leave."

Fazio glanced at Mancini. "An empty room is as a good place as any for a shootout."

Jonny turned to Fazio. "What do you mean by *shootout*?"

Fazio laughed. "Just a saying, Jonny . . . just an old saying."

As soon as they arrived at the restaurant, they cuddled under the wide, multicolored canopy. Then Fazio took the phone out of his pocket.

Seeing the phone, Jonny raised an eyebrow. "Who are you calling?"

"De Luca. He wants to be sure Garcia agreed to meet with us."

Jonny nodded then looked at his watch. "Seven-fifteen," he muttered.

Fazio stepped away from the others as he pushed a few buttons. "Piss poor connection. The canopy must be blocking the signal." Holding the phone in the air he stepped out into the rain. "I need to find a better signal somewhere."

Jonny shook his head in frustration. "Make it quick. Garcia should be here in a few minutes, and I don't want him to see all of you here."

After a few minutes of mumbled conversation, Fazio huddled back under the canopy and shook off the rain. "De Luca said he'll let the other Dons know about the meeting. He also wants you to know, regardless of how things turn out, Vallario said he was gonna take care of you for setting up the meeting."

Jonny took Linny aside. "I don't want Garcia to think I'm breaking his rules, so take everyone into the restaurant and make sure they spread out."

"What about you?"

"Don't worry about me, I'll be okay."

While everyone was scattering about inside the restaurant, Jonny waited outside under the broad canopy. Seven-thirty passed, no Garcia. Eight o'clock came; Garcia had not arrived. Jonny stepped out of the protection of the canopy into the drizzling rain long enough to look at the cars going up and down the narrow street. Still no sign of Garcia. Back under the comfort of the canopy, he looked at his watch again "Ten after eight! He should have been here by now. That's not a good sign."

Five minutes later, a black SUV pulled up in front of the restaurant. Jonny counted the men as they came out of the van. Jonny muttered, "Four soldiers . . . *Come alone* must be a one-sided rule."

The four men looked around then one blinked the SUV's headlights. Seeing the signal, another black SUV pulled up behind the first. The driver rushed out of the vehicle, opened a large umbrella, then helped Garcia out of the van.

"Senor Milano," Garcia said in his soft voice as he reached the restaurant door. "Sorry for being late."

"What happened to the *come-alone* rule?"

Garcia stepped towards Jonny. "Yes, the rule!" Looking around as if someone might be listening, he whispered,

"Senor Milano, like you big city gringos, we also have problems on this side of the border."

"I understand," Jonny said as they shook hands. "And I'm just an employee, so you can call me Jonny."

"Yes, Jonny . . . Senor Jonny," Garcia said as he pointed to the restaurant. "But let's get out of this rain first."

"Where do you want to go to discuss our *issues?*" Jonny asked.

"Ah, the issues . . . the important meeting. Best we use the de conferencias. But first, let me treat you to the best ceviche and tequila in Mexico."

Like I thought, the conference room. "Sounds good, but I ate earlier. Anyway, it looks like the restaurant is closing."

"Yes, the restaurant, well as the conferencias room, is closed to everyone but us," Garcia said as a dozen people were guided out by the soldiers. Jonny scoured the crowd to see if any of the four men he sent inside was in the crowd. They were not. *Where the hell did they go?*

Once the restaurant was emptied, Garcia pointed to a table in the back of the room. After a half-hour of small talk and a bottle of tequila, Jonny moved to the main subject. "Senor Garcia, everyone wants to make money. But to do this, there has to be some agreement between you and those I represent."

"Senor Jonny, you think . . . what is your word for raising a price?

"Jack up."

"Yes. *Jack up* . . . That we jack up the price of our product because we are greedy Mexicans?" Garcia continued as he pointed to his armed soldiers then back at Jonny. "But like

Don Vallario and your other amigos, we have people to pay, and to do that we must make a profit." After a long pause, He put his hand on Jonny's shoulder. "Senor Jonny, what is it you gringos say . . . *it gets harder and harder to--*"

"To *make ends meet?*" Jonny said."

"Yes, that's it, *to make ends meet.*" He took his hand from Jonny's shoulder. "So tell your boss, the price must remain, at least for now." Then his smile returned. "But things might change later. If they do, we will be more, as you put it, *flexible.*" After a long pause, Garcia continued but now with a glaring look. "Just to make sure there is no confusion, I will explain our position to your other *representatives* in a *manner* they will understand."

Jonny narrowed his brow. *How did he know they were here?* "Why would they be--"

Garcia just grinned. "Why would four men with guns be with you?"

Unable to come up with a believable answer to the unexpected question, Jonny struggled and settled for, "They rarely get out of New York, and . . . and this seemed a good time to look around your country. It must have been a mistake on my part."

Garcia flashed a closed-mouth smile. "I understand. You just misunderstood me when I said, *come alone.*"

"Where are they?"

Garcia patted Jonny on the shoulder. "Do not worry, Senor. Your amigos are comfortable in the conferencias room." Then he nodded to one of his men. The next thing Jonny felt was a gun pushing into the back of his head. Stunned, he was pushed out of the restaurant towards the closed door of the conference room. Once they entered the room, Jonny's puzzlement turned to fear. Mancini, Ricco, and Linny were standing against the wall while two of Garcia's soldiers were pointing guns at them. Fazio was standing at the far side of the wall. Mexicans.

"I came here to negotiate, not--"

"Yes, the negotiation. Do not worry, my friend. I believe you, but your amigos, well it seems they came with another purpose in mind."

"These men were told to wait for me in the restaurant. How . . . why are they here with guns pointed at them?"

Garcia looked at a shocked Jonny then at his men. Suddenly the room was filled with deafening blasts sending Francis Mancini, Joe Ricco, and his longtime friend, Linny Calabrese, onto the floor. Jonny and Fazio were left standing.

Jonny shouted, "Why?" as he headed towards Garcia until he was pulled back by two of the armed men.

"Since your Dons do not seem to want to negotiate, I am sending them a message . . . we're not in the mood to negotiate either."

"You were waiting for us. Who set us up?"

Garcia narrowed his brows and looked deep into Jonny's eyes and pointed to Fazio. "Ask your compadre who made the phone call."

Grabbing Fazio by his shirt collar, Jonny slammed him into the wall while shouting, "You! You and De Luca knew all along they planned to kill us,"

"You are right, Senor," Garcia said as he pointed his gun at Jonny. "Your amigo and his boss set you up," then his gun followed Fazio as he dropped to his knees. Trembling on the floor.

"Please! Please, Senor Garcia," Fazio begged "I helped you . . . I warned you they planned to kill you."

"Senior, Jonny, would you like me to kill this traidor for you or should I just leave him for the dogs?" When Jonny didn't answer, Garcia lowered his gun. "Don't worry, Senior Fazio. In Mexico, pinchie traidors like you are not worth the cost of a bullet." Laughing, he turned back to Jonny. "I'll leave your amigo for you to deal with."

After motioning to his men," he left leaving three dead men, a panicked traitor, and an angry Jonny behind him.

After Garcia was out of sight, Jonny grabbed Fazio by his shirt collar again and pulled him up from the floor. "Get out of here before I kill you myself."

"Jonny, I just . . ."

"Stay here or crawl back to the states," Jonny said as he pushed Fazio into the hall. "Either way, you're a dead man." That would be the last time he would see the traitor again . . . in one piece.

After grabbing his suitcase from his room, Jonny waved a taxi down. "To the Ciudad Airport," he said to the driver as he handed him a hundred-dollar bill. "And make it fast."

⸎ ❖ ❖ ⸎

Once he arrived at the airport, Jonny called Varrario. "You planned to assassinate Garcia all the time didn't you . . . using me as your frontman."

"Sorry, Jonny, but your negotiations were not getting anywhere," Vallario said in his soft *too bad* tone. "But don't take it personally. They would never have accepted our demand for lower prices anyway, and you, you would never have gone if you knew my plan." After a brief pause, Vallario continued. "Anyway, it's done."

"It's done alright, but not the way you planned," Jonny replied. "Only Fazio and I are left here; Mancini, Ricco, and Linny are dead."

Jonny could hear Vallario's deep breath over the phone. "What happened, Jonny?"

"Garcia knew what you were planning!"

"How could he have known?" Vallario shouted.

"Someone had to tell him," Jonny said in a less than respectful tone. "Since we were the only two Garcia let go, it had to be Fazio, but he wouldn't have the balls to do it without De Luca's blessing."

Vallario lowered his voice to his level. "Don't worry, Jonny. I'll take care of Fazio as well as De Luca."

"Don't try to appease me. It won't work. Taking care of the bastards won't matter to the three dead men I'm leaving behind."

"Jonny, you'll feel better about this once you get home."

Jonny took a deep breath. He didn't know where home was anymore, but he did know he could never return to his old life with the Company. He also knew that Vallario's promise of retaliation was just that, a promise. None of the Dons would make another Caporegime pay with their life for something they did unless they were threatened. Although he knew Linny and the others would never have justice, he felt he owed it to Vallario to give him a chance to make things right.

"I have to go now," he said in a softer voice, "but I need to see you when I get back—at your house, not the office."

❖❖❖

Jonny left Ciudad and headed toward El Paso International Airport. Once on the U.S. side of Highway 85, he decided he needed to calm down before he saw Vallario. Three days on the road, sleeping only a few hours a day in the rented van, and an eight-hour stop at a cheap motel, gave him plenty of time to think about what he would say to Vallario and put together a plan that would get him out of the *business*. He wasn't able to answer either one. After hours of deep thought, he realized the only thing he was sure about was that he had to get out of the *business*. After returning the rental van in the city, he grabbed a taxi and headed towards Manhattan and Don Vallario.

CHAPTER 5

Long before Alonzo Vallario was Don Vallario, he was an irrelevant migrate from Italy whose only skill was being acquainted with the money-making skills supported by the Mafia. This skill was not overlooked by Mafia Don, Stefano Bianchi. One evening, Bianchi took him aside. "Alonzo, I've watched you for over a year now. I believe you are ready to do more than the piccolo money-making truffa you run."

Alonzo was quick to agree. Not only did it line his pocket, but it also gave him status as a money collecter. Attached to this rise in rank was something even more important than status and money-- protection.

Soon his efficiency was rewarded by Don Bianchi with a *graduation* present. Alonzo Vallario was now armed with a 9 mm Luger, something he would treasure all of his life.

It was common to see Vallario strutting up the street in his broad-brimmed hat, waving at everyone he passed. Everyone waved back . . . fear demanded respect whether earned or not. This Saturday he was on his way to Andrea's Fine Foods.

"Ah, my friend, Andrea," he said as he looked over the artisanal cheeses and fresh deli meat. "How goes your business?"

Trembling, the elderly man wiped his hands on his apron and took a deep breath. "Lento, Senor Vallario, but I know it will pick up soon. Then I can pay you what I owe."

Vallario raised his hands and smiled. "Senor Andrea, it's not me you are paying, it is Don Bianchi. And when your business is slow, his business is slow. That is something neither of us can allow."

"I know, but--"

"We have been in business together for a long time, my friend. Because of that, I will give you another week. After that, friendship has to be put aside, and it will be difficult for me to protect you and your business."

"Senor Vallario, I can't pay you and the others at the same time for the same protection. I ask you, please talk to them. Maybe you can divide the money I gave them, then they'll go somewhere else. Then--"

"You paid someone else?"

"Yes! Two men. They said they worked for someone who could give me protection for less than you. At first, I told them no! I do business only with Don Bianchi. But that night, my windows were broken and almost everything of value was taken. I did not want to, but I had no choice but to pay them." Andrea lowered his head out of fear. "Regardless of who I pay, no one is going to protect me."

"Who were these men?"

"One was called Luca and the other was Sergio. That's all I know."

"Luca Esposito and his brother. I know them well. I will talk to them. I'm sure we can come to an agreement."

That night Luca and Sergio were coming out of a bar and heading home. As they turned into an alley, Vallario stepped out of the darkness, pointed the 9 mm at their heads, and pulled the trigger. The Don Bianchi and Andrea's problems were now taken care of. That was the beginning of his uprising in the Mafia.

On a wintry day in 1921, Bianchi and his apprentice, Vallario, were at a New Year's party with several other Dons. Laughter, wine, and stalking beddable women, soon turned to politics and how their businesses might be affected under a fascist government.

"If Benito Mussolini comes into power, he will close up all of our businesses," one Don warned.

"Worse, he will not hesitate to send his mobsters to corral us," Vallario added. "If that happens, prison would look like a vacation."

Bianchi shook his head. "Alonzo, you grieve too much about what may happen instead of what is happening. All Mussolini can do now is to make threats, and threats don't hurt us."

"Senor Vallario is right, Don Bianchi," another said as he joined the argument. "As fast as fascism is catching on, I would not underestimate this strutting bastardo."

"You all worry too much," Bianchi said as he pulled his woolen scarf closer to his neck. "Even if, by some miracle, the monster gains power, he'll close his eyes to the Mafia as long as we show support for him and let him wet his beak from our fountain. I tell you, he will set us aside and deal with the real problems left over from the war."

For one of the few times, Bianchi was wrong. By 1922, Mussolini's threats turned into action. While Don Bianchi was dying in an Italian prison, Don Alonzo Vallario was on a ship to New York.

⸺ ❖❖ ⸺

Vallario was sitting on a large chair facing Jonny when Jonny arrived at his mansion. "Jonny B, I don't usually discuss company business at my home because my phone and TV have been bugged several times. When your telephone breaks down or your TV fades out, you call someone to fix them. They sound like they know what they're doing, so you get careless and let them do their job. Later, you find out they left a bug somewhere. They're sneaky, those black-bag men with their little bugs. You gotta be careful these days. I flushed a couple of *bugs* out this week. I made sure everything is clean, so we can talk without any problem."

Jonny nodded, "I appreciate the courtesy."

"Jonny, I want you to understand, I didn't think things would go down the way they did in Mexico. I trusted the Dons just like I know I can trust you. Even when De Luca insisted on sending his man, Fazio with you, I trusted him. Who would know it would turn out like this. But I don't let it concern you. I will look into it."

"I understand, Boss, but what I want to--"

"I know what you want to do, Jonny . . . or what you want me to do. Believe me, losing those four men troubles me just as much as it does you. They were part of my family"

"Four?" Jonny said with a raised brow.

"Yes, four . . . when you add Fazio."

"Fazio was alive when I left him in Mexico."

"He didn't stay alive long."

"What happened to him?"

"This is just between you and me. I received a package from Mexico a few days after you came back. It was packed in hot ice."

"Hot ice! What would need that?"

"Fazio's head!"

"His head! My God! That makes De Luca even more guilty. Fazio was his puppet. He knew what the bastard Fazio was up to. Fazio wouldn't take a piss without his permission. For God's sake, De Luca needs to pay for it."

"That's for me to decide, Jonny, but if I find he was behind this he will pay."

"You know Fazio would not do something like this without the--"

Vallario's shout cut Jonny off. "Don't tell me what I know or don't know. Didn't you hear me? I said I will look into it. You need to leave it there. Everybody knows Fazio was a hot-head. He was a nutcase all of his life. This is on him, not De Luca, and he paid for it."

Vallario knew by Jonny's reaction that he was not listening to him. "Jonny, I understand your anger, but I assure you, the first De Luca knew about the massacre was when I met with him after you called me. He was surprised and denied knowing anything about what Fazio did or why he did it. But since one of his men acted without permission, he took the blame. All of the Dons agreed that a heavy financial penalty on De Luca was in order."

Jonny tightened his jaw and looked eye to eye with his boss. "A *financial* penalty? Are you kidding me? You should put De Luca's head in a basket for what he did."

"I was as angry as you until I realized the package from Mexico was meant to be a peace offering. That settled things for me."

"Or a warning," Jonny said.

"You've said enough. The issue is closed. Accept that." Vallario answered Jonny's sullen silence with a threatening glare. "Don't be your father, Jonny. Going off hot-headed without thinking things through was something he would do."

"I'm not my father."

"No, you're not. You think through a problem then come up with a solution. Mario was reckless, but he knew there were limits to my patience, and he never crossed that line. I respected him for that. He was the reason I've been lenient with you, letting you set limits about what you are willing to do and not do. Respect that line like your father did and don't step over it."

Vallario was right. Jonny was not prone to make rash decisions and apologizing later. However, the look on his face was the same look he had seen many times on the face of Mario Milano when he had already made his mind up. He also knew Jonny never carried a gun, but he knew where to get one and how to use it.

"My father isn't here to defend himself, so leave him out of it."

Vallario's face reddened. "I'm letting your arrogance and disrespect pass . . . this time because you haven't thought the Mexico fiasco through, but I'm warning you, how the De Luca issue gets handled is not your concern. Do you understand?"

Knowing he had stepped over the line, Jonny nodded.

"A nod is not an answer, *Mister Milano*. I want to hear you say you understand."

"Yes, Boss, I understand."

Vallario's angry eyes and flushing cheeks gradually faded. "Jonny, there will be a backlash from other Dons if I can't control my own *family*. If we want to keep the peace, we have to have limits." Vallario took a cigar out of his desk, bit off the end, lit it. After blowing a cloud of smoke in the air, he continued his lecture. "You need to understand that the who, what, or how is over your paygrade."

Jonny nodded. "You're right, we all have limits."

After a deep breath, Vallario regained his composure. "I'm glad you understand that because if I told the Dons what I think is floating around in your head, you would be dead. You know, *If De Luca, then why not one of us?* Forensic accountants are hard to find, Jonny. I don't want to lose mine."

"So, I have to forget the murder of my friend and the others?"

"Yes. That's the only option you have . . . if you don't want to join them." Another minute of quietness, another cloud of smoke, another glare, he continued. "So tell me you understand, and you'll let it go." Jonny didn't answer. That troubled Vallario. "You've been warned." Vallario waited again for a response. All he got was more dead air. "Okay, Mister Milano, unless you have something else to discuss, our meeting is over."

"No, sir. That's all I wanted to discuss."

CHAPTER 6

After leaving his meeting with Vallario, Jonny went to the Company's vault and grabbed documents containing financial transactions, transactions that would be difficult to explain if the FBI got hold of them. After putting what he considered to be *insurance* into his briefcase, he stopped by the Company's bank and headed towards a young lady busy thumbing through a file of papers at the desk buffering the manager's office. "I need to speak to Mister Conrad."

"Do you have an appointment?" the secretary asked without looking up.

"You must be new," Jonny said. "What's your name?"

"Janice, Janice Jones."

"Well, Miss Jones, I'm Jonny Milano, Mister Lonzo Vallario's accountant. If you ask Mister Conrad, you'll find I don't usually need an appointment, but--"

"I'm sorry, sir," she said as she quickly stood up. "I didn't know."

A minute later, the manager was shaking Jonny's hand then walked him to his office. "I'm sorry about the *appointment* thing, Mister Milano, but Miss Jones is new here." Once in the small office, he pointed to a leather chair. "Please sit down," he said while shuffling a pile of scattered papers. "And how is Mister Vallario doing?"

"Mister Vallario is doing just fine, Henry."

"Good to hear." After being satisfied that his desk was in order, he looked at Jonny. "Now what can I do for you and Mister Vallario?"

"Mister Vallario wants to open a new account then transfer three hundred thousand dollars into it. Put it in my name."

Henry raised his brow. "That's an unusual request, Mister Milano, and a lot of money, can--"

Jonny interrupted Henry, "Yes it is, at least for most people. Anyway, it's a family thing. You know, taking care of his grandkids."

"I didn't know he had grandchildren."

"Two actually, but he doesn't talk about them since they live with their grandmother. Like most spoiled kids, they don't know how to handle money, so he keeps a close eye on them . . . rather, makes sure I do." Handing Henry a notarized document, he continued. "Anyway, he gave me the honor of being the boys' financial keeper, like I don't have enough to do keeping up with his finances."

"I know about that," Henry said while looking at the document. "Got kids myself. Looking ahead for grandchildren. How about you?"

"None. At least none that I know of," Jonny said with a wide grin. "Anyway, I'll be their custodian until they learn that money doesn't grow on trees."

Henry shook his head. "Wish I had such grandparents."

Jonny laughed. "Me too. Yeah, one more thing. I want to change a few thousand into pesos . . . out of my account of course. Any problem with that?"

Henry smiled. "You going to Mexico?"

"Yes, I'm considering an investment there."

After the money transfer, as was his morning routine, Jonny stopped at a café a block away from the company office. "Good morning, Mister Milano," the waitress said as she put his cup of coffee on the table, like always, black with two sugars.

"Two eggs, sunny-side up, and three slices of bacon?"

"Just the coffee today, Betty."

After watching Betty's rounded buttocks swaying as she walked away, he put a twenty-dollar tip on the table, then looked at his watch. Time was pushing him. He had three more things to do: transfer money from the college account in New York to his account in New Jersey, put his *protection* documents in a safe deposit box in his Jersey bank, then see his attorney. After finishing his business in New Jersey, he headed back to his apartment with a cashier's check for two-hundred-thousand dollars made out to Carlene Sabella and another one-hundred thousand put in his new account.

❦ ❦ ❦

Jonny tried to sleep, but too many things kept him from indulging in that leisure. Tossing the useless pillow onto the floor, he went into the kitchen. Struggling to come up with a way to deal with De Luca, he went over one plan then another. Everything he came up with was complicated and each could be a life-changer one way or another.

"I never thought planning to . . ." then he hesitated. The word that was so familiar in meaningless conversations was now too difficult to say. Finally, he forced it out of his mouth . . . . "*kill* someone?"

Two coffees later, each tainted with an ounce of bourbon, he continued to argue with himself over the pros and cons of how to do what needed to be done.

Leaving my job suddenly without a good reason will bring an army of soldiers looking for me. Even if I come up with a reason to leave, De Luca will likely be barricaded in his mansion, making it impossible to get to him. If I survive that, I'll need to find a place to hide. Then there's the Mexico issue to deal with.

Looking into the bathroom's dust-smeared mirror, he saw a fatigued, conflicted, Jonny Milano. Closed eyes, trembling hands covering his face, he struggled to drive out the confusion rolling around in his head. After several minutes, he slammed the mirror closed and asked the question that troubled him most: *In the long run, how likely is it that I will stay alive?*

⬦ ⬦

It was early in the morning when he called Vallario. "Boss, I need to take some time off."

"Jonny B, you just had some time off."

"Seeing three men murdered, including my long-time friend, Linny, and the package you received, it didn't seem much like *time off*."

"Jonny, that thing in Mexico was unfortunate. But that's one of the risks in our line of business. Like I told you, it's closed. We're back in business as usual."

"Boss, I accept that you and the other Dons know best. The other guys know that as well. But I need--"

"You need what?"

"I don't know . . . just going somewhere quiet. Maybe back to the beach. I'd be just a shout away if you should need me."

Vallario remembered the *Mario Milano* look in Jonny's eyes. "I'm worried about you, Jonny. At my house last week you reminded me more of your old man. He often took things into his own hands. We all know how that turned out. I'd hate to see that happen to you."

"I'm not my dad, Boss. I won't make the same mistakes he made. I just need a few more days to clear my mind and think about things."

While Jonny left, thinking problem number one on his list was resolved, Vallario was asking himself if taking a chance with Jonny was in the *Company's* best interest. He decided it was not. Shaking his head in frustration, he picked up the phone and called Frenchie Durand. After he hung up, he muttered, "Jonny, it's not personal."

. . .

"We've got him," FBI undercover agent Randy Collins shouted from the disguised van parked two blocks away. Thank God for bugs. Now we can bring in RICO!"

"Don't jump the gun, Randy," Agent Ryan warned.

"Come on, Ann. We heard him."

"Yes, we heard him, and *we* know what he was ordering Durand to do. But he was very careful with his words. Careful enough that a good attorney could argue that he meant something else, and a jury would probably agree with him. No, we need to keep him bugged for a while longer. Who knows, he might lead us to a bigger fish."

CHAPTER 7

Sag Island had surrendered to the coldness of winter.
Most bars were closing or at best limiting their hours
of operation. He hoped Tucker's Tavern would still be
open; it wasn't, but Tucker was still there cleaning and
putting up what could be stored until spring.

Jonny's tap on the window brought Tucker to the door.
"Can't you see we're closed?" he grumbled.

"Do you remember me, Mister Tucker?"

Tucker squinched his eyes. "Humm--"

"I'm Jonny Milano? I was here recently on my vacation?"

Putting on thick glasses, Tucker looked Jonny over
again. "Yes, I do know you, son; at least my waitress knows
you. Come on in and have a shot on the house before it's
all put away."

"Can I help you get closed up and go home?"

"I'm already home," Tucker said as he pointed upward.
"I live up there. Makes life a lot easier."

Both men sat at the bar in front of a bottle of aged
bourbon. "Carlene talked about you a lot, Mister Milano."

"Call me Jonny," Jonny said with a smile. Then he realized he hadn't smiled in a long time. "I hope she said good things."

"The kid kinda liked you, but she wasn't sure about you, being an older man and all."

"Oh yeah, that bothered me, too, but I realized she was special."

"Well, you're a bit too late, son. She's gone for the season, but you might call her." Tucker said as he scavaged through a pile of papers. "I think I have her phone number." After a few minutes of grumbling, Tucker handed Jonny a piece of torn paper. "Here. I knew I had her number somewhere."

When Jonny stuffed the paper into his pocket and stood up to leave, Tucker motioned for him to sit back down. "Have another drink, Mister Milano--"

"It's Jonny, sir."

"Okay, Jonny. I got to get back to work, but no need for you to leave unless you got somewhere to be."

"Thanks, Mister--"

"No Mister's around here son, so just call me what everyone calls me . . . well maybe not what everyone calls me," he said with a laugh. "But Tucker will do just fine."

"I'm not in any hurry, Mister--"

"Tucker, young man."

"Sorry. . .Tucker, I have to make a phone call then I'll help you."

"No thanks, son. You go on with your phone call. I can do this. It takes a few days, but I know where everything goes."

When Jonny pulled out his cell phone, Tucker pointed to the bar. "Connection with those fancy phones ain't always good. You might want to use the phone over there."

Tucker was right, there was no signal, so he used the bar's phone and dialed a number. After several rings, a curt voice said, "Hello."

"Paulie, this is Jonny."

"Jonny!" Paulie said in a surprised tone, then with a whisper, he asked, "Where are you?"

"Same place as last time, Havens Beach. Taking care of some unfinished business."

Still whispering, Paulie asked, "What type of *business*, Jonny?"

Jonny laughed. "Personal business . . . not *Company* type of business."

"You calling shacking up with your girlfriend, *business*?"

"*My girlfriend?*"

Paulie laughed. "Yea. thanks to Linny, may he rest in peace, everybody knows about your girl at the bar."

"As usual, Linny was wrong. The bar is a tavern and *my girlfriend* is just a friend . . . nothing more. Anyway, since she's gone for the season, I think I'll drift farther down south for a day or two before I come back to work. I just wanted to check in to see how things are going in the city."

"Since you left, the *office* has been a bit stressed." After a pause, Paulie continued. "And a lot of people have *asked* about you, Jonny."

Paulie's words and tone were clear: *They're looking for you.* "I guess they miss me," Jonny said after a pause. "Other than me being *missed*, how is the *weather* there?"

"As you know, the weather doesn't answer to anything or anybody. When the sun's up you burn when it's not . . . hell, who knows."

"I don't want to be burned, so I'll stay out of the sun."

"That's a good idea, Jonny . . . although sunburns can be pretty bad, other things can be worse."

"What's worse than a sunburn, Paulie?"

"I hear rumors that a hurricane might be coming. . .that might be worse."

"I haven't paid much attention to the weather, so thanks for the heads up. Do me a favor, don't let anyone know where I'm at. If they know, they'll just drag me back to work. That would spoil my *vacation*."

"Nobody will hear it from me, but you never can . . . just be careful, you know how . . . " again, another unfinished sentence. "Just be careful." Still whispering, he added, "Jonny, I know we're not as close as you and Linny were, but he was my friend, too. I would never have been part of the Mexico thing. And considering the times you spoke up for me. . .especially when I had that issue with the drug dealers--"

"Don't go there!"

"I know, but still I owe you for that."

Paulie was right. Jonny had covered up for him the day Vallario sent both of them to get money from the drug dealers. When guns came out, Paulie backed off, but Jonny told Vallario the dealers left the city before they could get to them. After a long pause for his words to sink in, Paulie continued. "So I think going further south might be a good idea. That's what I would do."

Paulie's message was clear: *Vallario was going to make sure he did not do anything that would upset him and the other Dons.*

"Paulie, I appreciate your concern, and thank you more for the *advice*," Jonny said as he hung up.

He knew killing De Luca would eventually make him a marked man, but he didn't think it would happen before he threw the first blow. "I have to deal with it, but not now," he muttered then looked at the paper in his hand and dialed the phone number. After three rings, a familiar soft voice said, "Hello."

CHAPTER 8

Carlene's 800-sq.-foot home was small but immaculately clean. Over a cup of strong coffee, she took a deep breath, tilted her head, and looked at Jonny. "Long time, Jonny. How have you been?"

Jonny cleared his throat, put on the usual grin when he didn't know what to say, and mumbled, "Yea. Too long. I'm sorry, but--"

"No sorry needed. I know you're a busy man. Most accountants are. Anyway, that was yesterday. Let's just focus on today."

"I wish I could just focus on today, but I have a lot to tell you. Most of which are things that you might not want to hear."

"Try me. I hear a lot of horrible things working at the pub."

Jonny found Carlene to be someone he could confide in without being judged. She listened as he spelled out his less than acceptable job with a Mafia family.

"Carlene, I might be in a little trouble with my employer . . . and--"

"We all have employer issues at times. You should see the arguments Tucker and I get into, but we always get over it. I think--"

"I'm afraid mine might be the type of trouble you can't get over. I don't want you to get involved, but I need someone to talk to, and I might need a favor . . . a really big favor."

"I don't have a cross to bless you with, but how about another cup of coffee while you're making your *confession?*"

"You might need to spike it with a bit of bourbon," Jonny replied.

Carlene shook her head. "Sorry, but the bar is closed."

This brought a wide smile to Jonny's face. "You going to make me go through this cold turkey? Anyway, I've made a lot of bad decisions over the years, fraud, accessory after the fact, sometimes before the fact, bribing, and once or twice, extortion, to name a few. But I never killed anyone . . . that might soon . . ."

Carlene interrupted him then looked him in the eye. "I bet everyone has thought about killing someone at one time or another. But there's a big difference in thinking about doing something and actually doing it." After a long pause and a deep breath, she continued. "What would you think if I told you that I've thought about killing someone, or worse, that I did kill someone?"

"You killing someone? Don't be silly," Jonny said with a laugh.

Carlene looked deep into Jonny's blue eyes. "Maybe I am being silly, but you're sounding pretty silly yourself."

"Silly or not, that's my story." After a long pause and another eye-to-eye gaze, he smiled. "So if you want me to leave, just say so. I'll understand."

"More silly talk. Okay, so you work for a less than honest man who most people in my world would call a crook, and you tamper with files to make him look good. You're also angry over your friend being killed in Mexico, and you think you know who was behind it . . . you *think* you know, Jonny . . . *you think you know*! And you want to kill this, what's he called? Oh yea, this Don. I get it." Then she put her hand on his arm and smiled. "You can't change the past, Jonny. What's important is you want to change the future. Maybe I can help."

Jonnie pushed back Carlene's long dark hair and looked deep into her hazel eyes. "As I said, I don't want you involved in anything I'm involved in. Things I've done have consequences, consequences that I have to live with." After several minutes of quietness, he continued. "These are things I could never tell anyone. But somehow, I am comfortable telling you. At the same time, I know that telling you too much will make you wonder what kind of man I am."

Carlene finally put her finger over his lips. "I'm not a detective or FBI agent, but if they had enough evidence to charge you with the things you told me about, why haven't they arrested you by now?"

"Why? Because they don't want me . . . they want the bosses, and they think I'll turn on them if they harass me enough. Anyway, I just don't want you to get involved in my troubles."

Jonny did not go back to the hotel that night, and for the first time in years, he did not sleep alone. Carlene was still sleeping when the sun rose. Careful not to wake her, he kissed her forehead and got dressed, made a quick call to Paulie. Listening to the *change in the weather*, he decided to leave a note. As he was writing, Carlene came into the kitchen.

"Going somewhere?" she asked.

"I didn't want to wake you, but since I called you yesterday, things have changed. There's a chance that someone, FBI or worse, might be looking for me here. For your safety, I have to leave."

"I guess you're going back there then," she asked in a somber tone.

Although Jonny nodded, he had not yet decided where *back* was.

Carlene put her hands on his shoulders then gave him a gentle shake. "You know that's the first place they'll look for you." Her tone sounded more frightening than a warning.

Hoping he would reassure her, Jonny gently put his hands over hers. "I have to risk that since the business I have to take care of is there. But I promise you, I'm not going back to the life I've been living."

Carlene pulled away. "Well, at least we had one night together. I'm glad for that," she said with a distressing glare.

Jonny reached out for her hand. "Me too, but one night is not enough. What would you say if I asked you to go away with me?"

Carlene sighed. "I'd have to think about that for a few seconds, I guess," she replied with a closed mouth smile, then hugged him.

"After I finish my business there, I'll be back. We can discuss this issue then." Then he handed her the cashier's check. "This should hold you over for a while."

"Jonny, I don't want your money . . . I just want you."

"Just look at it as a loan or payment for all you've done for me and what I am going to ask you to do." Then he handed her a card. "The *thing* everyone is after is in a safe deposit box. Only my attorney knows where."

"Can't you tell me?"

"No. If they think you know, that would put you in even more danger." He took a deep breath then continued. "I don't want you involved any deeper than you are now, but if anyone should contact you asking about me, that will be your cue to contact the FBI." He handed her Agent Ryan's card then wrapped his arms now around her and whispered, "I'm so sorry you got wrapped up in my problems. Had I known, I--"

Carlene pulled back and put her finger over his lips. "Jonny B, it's okay. I'm a big girl, so don't worry about me. Thanks to Tucker, I can take care of myself."

"Tucker?"

"Yea. I was sliding down a muddy hill when the old man took me in. He was more like a grandfather than an employer. Although he would never admit it, he turned my life around."

As he drove back to the city, Jonny thought about what Carlene said: *Thinking about killing someone was a lot easier than actually killing someone.* However, it was not difficult for others, especially not for Durand.

CHAPTER 9

As Jonny arrived back in the city, the clouds darkened. Heavy rain, deafening roars of thunder, and bolts of lightning followed as if they were warning omens. Soon he was forced into a motel in the slummy part of the city. Its name, *Duffy's Inn*, fit its appearance.

"How long you gonna stay," the beady-eyed clerk asked as he looked up from the *For Men Only* magazine.

"A few hours," Jonny replied. "Just enough to let the rain stop."

The clerk pushed a sign-in book across the shielded cage then turned back to his girly magazine as if someone might jerk one of the nude girls away from him if he wasn't watching them.

Without looking up, the clerk mumbled, "Cost the same, overnight or a few hours," then looked up long enough to tell Jonny "Cash or card, Mister--"

"Rogers!" Jonny replied. "John Rogers, and cash."

After counting the money, the clerk handed him a key from a board full of keys, evidence that only a few, if any, of the rooms were filled. "Room 323 on the third floor."

Eyes back to the magazine. "Gonna have to take the stairs, the damn elevator's not working."

After checking in, Jonny sat down in the shaggy chair in front of the television and took a deep breath. "Not the Four Seasons, but it's not likely anyone will be looking for me here." After he pushed the smutty room out of his mind he focused on what he had to do. Getting a gun would not be a problem, but everything that followed could . . . would be a problem. He spent the next three hours tossing his options over and over, asking questions that had no answer. He decided to address one issue at a time. First getting a gun, next, finding a way to isolate De Luca in a building harboring a dozen or more guards.

*Okay, I'm showing up at night alone, without the blessing of my boss, to offer another Don a briefcase full of his competitor's company files. . .*then he smiled. *De Luca would grab the opportunity to stab Vallario in the back.* Suddenly, the smile turned into a frown. *Even if I manage to get the bastard alone long enough to shoot him, how do I get away alive afterward?*

He shook his head and muttered, "Getting him alone will work, the other. . .that's something else!" He left the chair and went to the smudged window that gave a full view of the dark alley, garbage cans, and two men sitting under a wobbling awning. The rain had given away to clear skies and a full moon. He looked up at the moonlit sky. "Maybe that's a good omen?" Then he flopped onto the swagging bed. A *few hours* turned into *overnight*.

Just as the sun was rising over the Big City, Jonny made a phone call. Two hours later, Tucker knocked on his door. "Sorry I took so long, Mister Jonny."

"I'm sorry I woke you up so early, Tucker."

"No problem. I was up hours before you called." Opening a cloth bag, he handed Jonny an ancient Colt revolver. "This was the best I could come up with. Had it a long time and never had to use it." After spinning the cylinder several times, he opened a box of 38 shells. "In case you need more than the five in it already."

"Thanks. I owe you a lot for not asking why I wanted it."

"I learned a long time ago, Son, *why* gets you in a lot more trouble than just *giving.*" He handed the gun to Jonny, patted him on the back, and whispered, "I hope you never have to use it, but if you do, I know you enough to know it will be for a good cause."

After Tucker left, Jonny decided the motel was as good a place to hide as any, then he paid the grumpy clerk for another day.

⊰⊱ ◆◆ ⊰⊱

Durand arrived at Tucker's Tavern only to find the bar closed. "Damn it," he said as he banged on the door the third time.

As he was walking away in frustration, Tucker stepped out onto the small balcony and looked down at the stranger banging on the tavern door. "What's all that hammering about," he shouted. "Can't you read? I'm closed for the season."

Durand looked up and waved. "You Mister Tucker?"

"Like I tell everybody, there ain't no Mister Tucker . . . just Tucker. What business you here for?"

"Not here for any business. Just want some information."

"What do you want? Directions to somewhere?"

"No, I just need--"

"Other than directions, I don't have much information worth anything to anybody."

"I think you can help me. Can I come up there? It might be worth your time . . . financially that is."

With money being involved, Tucker motioned for Durand to come upstairs. Once Durand stepped onto the balcony Tucker looked him over. He sensed something about the giant's sullen face and leering eyes that he didn't like. "What is it you want, Mister--"

Instead of answering, Durand put his hand on Tucker's shoulder and said, "Let's go inside to talk."

Tucker pushed the hand off his shoulder. "No need to go inside. Just tell me what you want that's so important?"

Durant grabbed Tucker's arm again, this time squeezing and demanding. "Old man, I said let's go inside."

Tucker's first judgment of the huge man was confirmed; he was a man that few liked and many feared.

Once inside the small home that consisted of a bathroom, a kitchen, and a small living room that served as a bedroom as well, Durand pushed him against the wall. "We can do this either the easy way or the hard way, old-timer. It's up to you."

"Mister, I don't have no money or anything of value except my bar downstairs and it won't get me anything until I open up again in a few months."

"I'm not after your money, old man. I just want answers to a few questions. Give me the right answers and I'll be on my way."

Being a bartender, Tucker didn't scare easily. Many drunks in his bar learned that. However, the man now holding a gun at his head was not the usual man who needed alcohol to bring out his bravery and anger. "What do you want to know?"

"I'm looking for a man. Tall, dark skin with blue eyes. His name is Jonny."

"I don't know anybody by that name or looks like that . . . honest, Mister."

Durand's other hand grabbed Tucker by the throat. "Don't give me a bag of bullshit. He was in your bar just a day ago and made at least two calls. Where did he go?"

"It ain't a bar, it's a tavern," Tucker said with pride. "And a lot of folks make calls from there."

"Not when you're closing. And if they did, they don't have the phones on the other end tapped by the NYC cops that share everything with us."

Fear was growing as Tucker nodded. "I remember now, he was here. And he did make a phone call, but I don't know who he called."

"He would have called his girlfriend. You know, your hired help."

"I don't know anything about a girlfriend or hired help. It's just me--"

"You're lying, old man," Durand shouted.

"It's just me, I told you. I don't have any help."

"Do you think I'm stupid?" Durand asked as he pushed his gun harder against Tucker's head. "I asked the lady up the street if anyone worked for you. She said a girl worked here. So, don't be stupid, tell me where she is or--"

"She was just part-time help, but she was already gone when he came in." He felt the gun pushing harder into his head. "Okay, maybe, he did call her, he didn't say. He just made his calls then left. Honest, I don't know where he went."

"She would know where he is," Durand muttered. "Give me her phone number or I'll splatter your brain all over this petty dump you call home."

Tucker knew what he just heard was a death warrant. "Mister, I'm just a bartender. I don't get into other people's business, and I know how to keep my mouth shut. Nobody will know what you just said or that you were even here . . . I swear."

"Just tell me where the girl is, and we'll part company without anybody getting hurt," Durand said as he moved his hand from Tucker's neck and backed away.

Tucker made several deep breaths. "It's like the lady down the street said, but she was just passing through and wanted some part-time work."

"Where does she live?"

"She rented a small house a few miles from here, but she never said where." Tucker grimaced at Durand's look as his hand pulled him closer to his face. Self-survival was now in total control. "But she left a here a few days ago. Maybe going back to Georgia. I don't know. But she's likely gone by now."

"Where in Georgia?"

"I'm not sure . . ."

"Think hard about it, old man," Durand said as he pushed his gun back against Tucker's shaking head.

Tucker took a deep breath and closed his eyes. His life or her life. Self-survival won. "Clayton I think . . . yeah, Clayton, Clayton Georgia."

"Where in Clayton?"

"Honest, she never said. Just Clayton."

"Do you have a picture of her?"

"No . . . I don't think so."

Durand pushed the gun deeper into his head. "You better think hard."

"Yes, yes. I got one. Her and the man you're looking for took it at the beach. Let me get it."

Hand grabbing the back of his shirt, Durand followed him. After looking into a cluttered drawer, Tucker pulled out the picture of Carlene and Jonny at the beach.

Durand lowered his gun and pushed Tucker away while looking at the picture. "That wasn't very hard now was it? Now give me her phone number."

Tucker nodded and pointed to the phone on the side table. "My phone book is over there. Her name's Carlene, Carlene Sabella. Her number is there."

One eye on Tucker and one on the phone book, Durand called the *Office*. After several rings, Paulie answered the phone. "What!"

"It's me," Durand said. "I know where the girl might be. Ask the boss what he wants me to do when I find her."

After waiting a few minutes, Vallario was on the phone. "What do you think I want you to do when you find her? Do what you do best or don't come back."

After slamming the phone down, Durand turned and pointed his gun back towards Tucker. "I hate people who squeal on their friends, old man." With a crooked, closed-mouth smile, he pulled the trigger. Now focused on getting to Carlene before she left for Georgia, he pushed Tucker's dead body aside and picked up the phone.

⬦ ⬦ ⬦

Carlene ignored the ringing phone out of fear of the unknown she was experiencing. Hoping that it was Jonny, she overcame her fear and picked up the phone. "Jonny?"

"Sorry, Miss Sabella. It's not your lover boy."

Her first instinct was to hang up the phone, but she was beginning to accept the unknown. "Who is this?"

"Just a friend of Jonny's. He wouldn't be there by any chance, would he?"

Knowing that Jonny had few friends left, none of whom would know to call her home, she asked again. "Who are you, and what do you want with him?"

"You can call me Frenchie, Carlene. If Jonny is there, let me talk to him. If he's not, it would be beneficial for you to tell me where I can find him."

"I haven't seen him for over a month or so. I assumed he was back at his job in the city. Other than that, I can't help you."

Durand's tone changed. "You know better than that. So put this social crap aside and listen to me if--"

82

"I said--"

"Don't interrupt me. I am in no mood to play games. Your lover boy took something from my boss. He wants it back."

"Mister Frenchie, or whatever your real name is, I can't help you so just leave me alone."

"Maybe we can make a deal. The money for the company books."

Her fear grew, and she started to hang up but what might follow kept her talking. "What money?"

"I said no games. Your Mister Milano stole three-hundred-thousand dollars from my boss. Knowing the gentleman he is, he would not have kept it when his girl needed it. But not to worry. You can keep the money if you tell me where Jonny boy is so I can get my boss's books back."

"I don't know anything about any *books* much less that much money, and I don't know where Mister Milano is, so I'm going to hang up now."

"That would be a big mistake. If I was able to get your phone number and a wonderful picture of you at the beach in that skimpy swimming suit, it wouldn't take long to find out where you live."

Carlene knew he was right. "Okay! He did give me some money . . . and your books." The lie about the books brought a buoyant look to Durand's face. "The money is important to me; your stupid books are not. So I accept your offer; the books for the money."

"If you decide to tell me where Jonny boy is," Durand said with a soft tone now, "I might add a few more dollars to what you have."

"I told you, I don't know where he is."

"Give me your address. You can think this over while I drive there."

"No!" I don't need to think about it!"

"What do you mean, no?"

"I mean, I don't trust being alone with you. So, we'll meet somewhere there are people. Then you can have what you want."

"You're smarter than I thought," Durand said. "Okay, but I don't know this place. You tell me where."

"Where are you now?"

"At Tucker's place."

"Let me talk to him."

"It seems Mister Tucker had an accident."

"Is he okay?"

"*Okay* depends on if he's a church-going man or not."

"What do you mean?" No answer. "Is he there?"

"He is here, but he's not in any condition to entertain company."

"What do you mean?"

"I'm sorry to be the carrier of bad news, but the poor man's accident was somewhat fatal."

Carlene gasped. "What did you do to him." It wasn't a question but an accusation. It was then that she realized the danger she was in, too. Trying to regain her posture, she sighed. "There's a small restaurant called Fanny's

Diner two blocks away from Tucker's place. I'll be there in an hour."

After hanging up, she searched for the card Jonny gave her. *Call this number if you think you're in any trouble.* She quickly dialed the number. After several rings, a woman answered. Hearing Carlene's story, she said, "You need to talk to one of our agents. Make sure you're safe where you are. If so, stay there. Someone will call you back in a few minutes."

While she was waiting, Carlene thought about her life and the changes she had little control over. Then the phone rang. "Misses Sabella, this is Agent Ryan."

Thirty minutes later, Carlene was in her car heading west, leaving Durand alone in Sag Island.

CHAPTER 10

Nightfall brought with it a cloudy sky with threats of rain. "So much for omens," Jonny said as he picked up the phone. After several rings, De Luca answered with a sharp, "Hello!"

Jonny struggled to cover his anger. "Don De Luca, this is Jonny Milano." All he could hear was De Luca's deep breaths. "Sir, this is Jonny--"

"I heard you the first time. What does Vallario want now?"

"Nothing. He doesn't know I'm calling."

"What the hell do--"

"I know, calling you without Don Vallario's permission is out of order. But knowing the consequences of bypassing him should tell you that what I want to talk to you about is not only important, but it is in your interest as well. That's why I don't want to discuss it over the phone. You never know who is listening."

De Luca's voice softened. "Mister Milano, you are treading on thin ice, but if what you have to tell me is, as you say, is in my *interest*, there's no reason anyone else should know about it. I'll see you at my house in, say three hours. Come alone."

After hanging up the phone, Jonny put the 38 caliber magnum Tucker gave him into his briefcase then went to the Company vault. "It's now or never," he said as he placed the Company's books on top of the gun.

When he arrived at De Luca's four-story mansion, he was greeted by two of De Luca's soldiers, Roscoe Randolf and his brother, Gordon. "I was glad to hear your dad was out of jail, Roscoe," Jonny said as he raised his arms. "How's he doing?"

"Doin' good," Roscoe said as he frisked him. Then he pointed to the briefcase. "Gotta see what's in the case, Jonny B."

Jonny opened the case enough that the stack of papers was obvious. When Roscoe reached to pick them up, Jonny gently closed it. "These documents are for Don De Luca's eyes only, Roscoe. I wouldn't touch them if I were you."

Gordon looked at his brother and shrugged his shoulders and moved away. "The Don is waiting for you, Jonny B."

As Jonny was escorted to the mansion by the Randolf brothers, he scanned the grounds that appeared to be never-ending. "Wow, this place makes my boss's house look shabby."

"Wait until you see inside. You'll think you're in the King of England's palace."

"Roscoe punched his brother in the shoulder. "Gordon, it's the *Queen* of England, not the *King* of England."

"King or Queen, I don't care. It's still a palace," Jonny said.

Once inside, he was escorted to an elevator that took him to the second floor where guards Georgio and Carson were arguing about who was the best fighter, Foreman or Frazier. "Damn, it Carson, Frazier is no match for a street fight, much less in the ring with Foreman." Before Giorgio could answer, he saw Jonny and his two escorts.

Roscoe pointed to Jonny. "The boss is waiting for him."

"You frisk him?" Carson asked as he pointed to Jonny and his briefcase.

"Of course he's clean. We know our job."

Jonny closed his eyes briefly. *Jonny B, shooting a Don is high on the list of stupid things to do; doing it in his living room with two guards outside the door, and God knows how many more in the building and on the grounds, then expect to get away alive, put it number one on the list.* Then he opened his eyes and took a deep breath. *Too late to back out now.*

De Luca answered the knock on the door with, "Send him in." Once Jonny was inside, De Luca pointed to an overstuffed chair and said "Sit." The pitch of his voice was more demanding than courteous.

Jonny sat down in the chair that would under other circumstances have been very comfortable, then set his briefcase on the floor. After a few minutes tapping his finger on his desk, De Luca broke the silence. "Jonny B, I'm an impatient man, so tell me, why are you here?"

Jonny swallowed while listening to the governing voice in his head: *Is this worth dying for? It's not too late to pick up the case and walk away. Just apologize to the ass for bothering him, and give him some bullshit reason for asking for the meeting. He might get pissed off and have you kicked out onto the street, but isn't that better than being carried out?* "No!"

"No, what?" De Luca asked with a confused look on his face.

"Sorry sir, just thinking out loud," Jonny answered.

"Don't waste my time with your thinking and tell me why in the hell are you here."

Jonny had been considering the *pick-up your case and walkout* option. De Luca's arrogance changed everything. Instead, he picked up his case and snuggled it in his lap. Then he opened the case and pulled out the documents.

"Is what you think I need to know in there?"

"Yes, but first let me ask you a couple of questions."

"In my *office*, I usually ask the questions, but I'll make an exception this time. Then show me what you in the have in the case that is so important to me."

Ask the question and the gate is closed behind you—there will be no turning back. He saw Linny falling to the floor with a bullet in his head along with two others he knew, and heard Vallario dismissing their deaths with a financial punishment on De Luca. "Why did you let Garcia kill those men?"

"That's what you came here for?"

Jonny's answer was in the case. He opened it and reached under the papers, and pulled out the revolver. Eyes wide open, De Luca looked at the gun pointing at him. "Milano, put that thing away," he muttered as he moved his hand towards the edge of his desk.

"I wouldn't do that if I were you."

"Are you crazy? If you do something stupid, you'll never get out of here alive."

"Maybe not, but touch that *panic button* under your desk and you'll never know because you'll be dead before anyone outside even sees the blinking light on the wall."

De Luca pulled his hand back. "Listen, Jonny--"

"It's time for you to listen...time for you to be held accountable."

"Accountable for what?"

"Accountable for setting us up in Mexico. Tell me, was it worth the money from Mexico to kill them?"

"It wasn't about the money, it was about--"

"Like Mencken said W*hen anyone says it's not about the money, it's about the money.* But maybe setting us up in Mexico was more for power than money."

"Listen, I never thought it would turn out like--"

"Like it did? How did you think it would turn out?" A long pause, then, "What did you think Garcia would do after Fazio told him they were there to execute him? You didn't care! You wanted power, regardless of the consequences."

"I'm telling you the truth."

"The truth is, you sacrificed Mancini, Ricco, and my friend, Linny, three men, just to get a monopoly on Garcia's drug business. So don't give me that *I didn't know* crap . . . you had to know."

De Luca's face raged with anger. He had never been talked to this way before.

"Jonny B, I had nothing to do with the Mexican tragedy. It was likely your boss . . . maybe one of the other

Dons. But it wasn't me." De Luca wiped away the sweat building on his brow. "Listen to me, Vallario has blood on his hands, too."

"Yea, his hands were bloodied when he sent us to Mexico to kill Garcia. He used me knowing Garcia would trust me, *the negotiator*. But his plan backfired, thanks to *your* messenger, Fazio."

"Fazio betrayed us all. He did what he thought would be to his advantage." He paused hoping Jonny would buy his lie. "Jonny, we can work this out if you just put that thing away and--"

"There's nothing to work out."

"Okay, Jonny. I knew about it, but it wasn't just to control the drug traffic. It was bigger than that. The bosses needed to see that I knew what to do, what had to be done, to solve our issues with the Mexicans. All Vallario worried about was his move up the ladder . . . up the ladder to bigger things."

"Bigger than being a Captain?" Jonny asked.

De Luca nodded. "A lot bigger . . . a Underboss. Think about it. Vallario has to have the fix in, Jonny, He was always old-school, and now he's even weaker. He wants to keep things going smoothly, but you can't build a business if you're seen as being weak. That's why the Mexican cartels are pushing us around. He needs to retire or *be retired*. Then the bosses would see that I have what it takes to get things done. I would be an Underboss. Then you could replace Vallario. You could be a Captain then . . . with my help."

"A power grab . . . at the cost of how many men?"

"A strong leader gets things done. Sure, someone has to pay at times. Just like Fazio paid."

"I'm not for sale. I just want to make you pay."

"There's no reason for you or me to pay for anything, Jonny." A long pause and another wipe of his forehead. "This is a big chance for you—a big chance for us." Another pause. "Mexico is yesterday's news. It can't be changed, so let it go."

"Tell that to the dead men left in Mexico."

"Jonny, it wasn't personal, it was just business."

"You can consider this as *just business*," Jonny said shaking knowing it was now or ever to pull the revolver's trigger. De Luca's head snapped backward then forward, splashing blood over his mahogany desk. He was still quivering when De Luca's guards rushed into the room. They ignored Jonny at first and ran to the bleeding man bent over in the chair behind his desk. Only then did they turn to Jonny, but it was too late. Jonny had his revolver pointed at them before they could draw theirs.

"What in the hell have you done, Milano?" Gorgie shouted.

Jonny waved his gun and pointed to chairs on the far side of the room. "Sit there." Reluctantly, both men obeyed. "I don't want to hurt you, but I will if I have to. So be quiet and listen to me. De Luca betrayed all of us when he sent Fazio to Mexico to tell Garcia that Vallario planned to kill him, not to negotiate. I was just a puppet. He knew the Mexicans knew me and would be at ease." Then he pointed to De Luca. "He wanted to make a deal with the Mexicans so he would have a monopoly with their drugs regardless of the price." Jonny lowered his gun and pointed to De Luca again. "He sacrificed Linny and the others for power, even if it meant a war between the Dons."

"None of that matters, Jonny," Gorgie said. "You killed a Don. They won't forgive you for that."

"Gorgie's right," Carson said. "You're a walking dead man."

"I knew that when I came in here."

"What now? Will Carson and I be next?" Gorgie asked.

"No. I don't want to hurt anybody else. All I want is a ten-minute headstart before you come after me. You can lay on the floor looking like I hit you. If I get caught, I'll say the same thing."

"There is no *if*, Jonny. If they could kill Kennedy, they would have no problem killing you."

Carson looked at Gorgie who nodded. "Ten minutes, Jonny. That's all. After that, you're fair game!"

"Understood."

It took Jonny just a few minutes to leave the house. When he reached the patio leading to the gaited grounds, Roscoe stopped him. "What was that noise upstairs?"

"He didn't like what I was telling him. He went into a rage, throwing whatever he could get his hands on, and kicked me out. I wouldn't go up there if I were you."

Michael laughed. "Thanks a lot! We're all going to catch hell now."

Jonny forced a laugh. "Sorry, but he'll get over it." Then he walked towards his car. "Better open the gate and let me get out before he yells for me to come back." With only minutes left, he passed the double gaits and headed for the highway.

⊷ ❖ ❖ ⊶

Vallario's phone rang an hour after De Luca was shot. He rubbed his eyes and looked at the clock beside his bed. Then he jerked the phone onto his bed. "Hello!"

"Mister Vallario--"

Vallario recognized the high-pitched voice. "Yes, Lieutenant!"

After a few deep breathes the NYC Police Lieutenant continued. "We just got a call that Angelo De Luca was murdered an hour ago. Shot in the head in his home."

This time it was Vallario who needed a deep breath. "I already know about it, Kaminski."

"Then you know who killed him?" After a long pause, Kaminski asked, "Did you hear me?"

Vallario reached for the bottle of bourbon sitting next to his box of Cuban cigars on the table next to his bed. "Yes! I heard you," Vallario said as he opened the bourbon.

"One of your boys taking him out, then walking out of the building without being stopped, doesn't look good for you."

Shaken for a minute, Vallario tossed down a deep class of bourbon as he thought about a Jonny B running loose after killing a Don. *Jonny, you stupid son-of-a-bitch. You just couldn't let it go.* More concerning, however, was could he be the next Don on Jonny's list. Putting the thought aside, he shouted at the NYC cop, "That's my problem, not yours!"

"Better yours than mine. I have a blind eye when it comes to your business, but you Dons are always surrounded by men, so how could anyone get that close to De Luca without inside help. I'm just saying, he might go after you next, so be careful. I can send a few of my men to protect you?"

"No! I want *every* cop in New York City looking for that stupid--"

"Don't worry. He's priority number one."

"Just keep me informed. I'll see that you get taken care of."

◈◈◈

It was close to midnight when Jonny reached Duffy's Inn. By now, every Don would know about De Luca. By morning there would be dozens of soldiers looking for him. With their contacts, they would eventually find him.

Vallario was especially concerned, but not because De Luca was killed. His departure was a gift since it removed one more candidate for promotion to a higher status. Silently, he thanked Jonny for that. However, any benefit from De Luca's departure was overshadowed with fear that he might be next on Jonny's list. He could not take that chance.

While Jonny was struggling with his next move, Vallario was holding a conference with the other Dons. The outcome of the meeting was not *if* to put a ransom on Jonny Milano's head, but *how much*.

After leaving the meeting, Vallario called his soldiers into his office. "Twenty-five grand to whoever brings Jonny B's head to me, dead or alive."

Durand left the meeting confident that he knew where Jonny would be hiding out. If not there, he knew there was someone who would know where to find him.

CHAPTER 11

Despite not having slept all night, the sun still rose. Jonny tossed all of his belongings in the handbag he brought with him and sat on the bed starring at them. As he left the bed, he looked at himself in the smudged mirror in the bathroom. "Jonny, you got yourself in a hell of a mess. Where can you go now?" he asked himself in a whisper. "Where to now!" he repeated, this time in a desperate tone. Although *where he could go* was not answerable, *where he could not go* was clear. Most important was avoiding places that would put his few friends in danger. Carlene's house was the first on his shortlist; Tucker's place was next. *You better make a decision soon. They'll be looking everywhere, including this place.* "Maybe not!" he said aloud as he picked up the phone. Then he hesitated for a few minutes. "Hell, I have nothing to lose."

❖ ❖

Vallario was surprised when he picked up the phone and heard the man he was looking for on the other end of the line. "After all you've *accomplished*, Jonny, I'm surprised to hear from you. So, what can I do for you?"

"It's what I can do for you, Mister Vallario . . . or what I won't do."

"Jonny B, you're sounding like your father again. In the end, he thought there wasn't anything I could do to him. Then he went wild."

"When will you learn that I'm not my father. But I won't argue with you over a dead man. What I want to tell you is, I want this to be over--"

"Sorry! There's nothing I can do to help you, but--"

"Don Vallario, despite your greed and sending me and four soldiers into a lion's den on a phony mission, I don't have any plans to go after you or anyone else. Just leave me alone. That's all I ask."

"Didn't you hear me? I warned you to let things go. You ignored me. There's a big bounty on your head, dead or alive. You're a dead man whether I find you or someone else finds you."

"As I said, I'm not my father. I plan."

Vallario's voice changed. He knew his accountant was smarter than people gave him credit for. "I'm listening."

"Check your vault, the one with the company books."

A long pause on the other end of the phone then, "Jonny, remember whatever you did, the books were *your product*."

"I see them as a life insurance policy."

"You don't need life insurance if you just bring them back."

"How safe would I be? As safe as my dad was?"

"Jonny, I liked Mario, just like I like you. I swear, I didn't have anything to do with his disappearance, but we can talk about your father if you come back."

"It's too late for that."

"No, it's not. I promise everything will be okay. I'll even straighten things out with the other Dons." Another long pause. "Trust me. It's the only option you have if you don't want to be a dead man."

"Trust you? I don't think so. Remember, I know the system. Forgiveness is not part of it. But I can give you an option. Forget about me. If you don't, the only options you leave me with are either going to jail or going six feet under? That, sir, will not be a hard decision."

"Going to jail . . . for what?" Vallario asked. "Turning over the books to the feds? That sounds like a threat. You need to remember, you're not the only one I can go after."

"Who's making threats now? Believe me, there's no one else involved in this."

"Don't try to bluff me, Jonny. I guess you haven't watched the news, so let me update you. It seems her boss, what was his name? Oh yeah, Tucker something. Anyway, it seems Mister Tucker had an accident. Shot himself in the head, so Durand said. But before Durand could stop him, the old man talked a lot . . . mentioned he knew your girlfriend's name and her phone number. Even had a picture of you and her on the beach. Gotta say, you might not have good judgment when it comes to betraying your friends here in the city, you have good taste in women."

Jonny sighed and closed his eyes. *Another thing to feel guilty about.* His voice now filled with anger, he shouted. "The old man was just a barkeeper. He didn't know anything about the Company's *business*. And as for the girl, she is just an acquaintance, not my girlfriend or anyone else's as far as I know. Even if she was more than that, I would think you'd be man enough not to play the *girlfriend* card. I should have known better, but I guess I overestimated your integrity."

"Come off the insults, Jonny. It's not your style. Still, I'm sorry about Mister Tucker's accident, but sometimes things just happen."

"Enough of your cloaked threats. I'm a few steps ahead of you. I added my *girlfriend* to my insurance policy. I suggest you are the one who needs to be concerned about *things happening*."

"Is that another threat, Jonny?"

"No! It's a promise!"

"You're smart, Jonny. I always knew that, so don't make promises you can't--"

Before Vallario could finish, Jonny interrupted him. "I'm smart enough not to make promises I can't keep, and I was smart enough to *borrow* a small retirement benefit from the Company's bank account. Just enough to get me started in a different profession."

"Then you'll die a rich man."

"Killing me would be a big mistake on your part."

"I don't make mistakes, Jonny. You should know that by now."

"Mexico was a mistake!"

"Maybe, but we need to talk about your mistakes. The biggest of which was that you stole from me."

"Stole? Maybe in *your* eyes." After a long pause, Jonny continued. "Stolen or not, they're in a safe place."

"Safe where?" Not expecting an answer to his question, Vallario was surprised when Jonny gave him an answer.

"Safe in a safe deposit box."

"Where might that be?" Vallario asked.

"Could be a lot of places, New York, Jersey, Ohio; do I need to go on? What you can be sure of is, if you harm her, I'll make sure the feds know where they are. Even if you get lucky enough to get me, I have an attorney who knows what to get, where to get it, and what to do with it. So coming after us would be another mistake and likely your last."

⬤━━ ✦✦ ━━⬤

After finishing his conversation with Vallario, Jonny turned his attention to the Mexican drug lord, Garcia, and Linny's murder. As his anger turned to rage, he mumbled, "For now, everything else has to be put on the shelf. Garcia is now at the top of my list. The big question is, how do I get close to him, much less close enough to kill him? After pouring a glass of bourbon, he sat in the sagging, overstuffed chair and turned on the evening news. It was then his life changed.

Early today a fatal car accident on Interstate 495 a few miles from Sag Island resulted in the death of Carlene Sabella, a Sag Island resident. The police report stated that the twenty-four-year-old woman fell asleep at the wheel and ran off the road hitting a telephone pole. She had no relatives in New York.

It took an hour and a bottle of bourbon before he could recover from the shock that he would never see Carlene again. Worse, he struggled with the guilt that he had pulled her into the world he was struggling to get out of. Although he couldn't prove it, his instinct told him Carlene's *accident* was *no accident* – Vallario had something to do with it. If so, holding onto the books did not protect her, and they would not protect him. Guilt turned to anger as he picked up the phone and called his attorney.

"Mister Roberts, this is Jonny Milano. You remember that package I put in the safe deposit box in Jersey, the one you have access to?" Roberts said he did. "Then I need a favor. Pick it up and send it to FBI agent, Ann Ryan at 26 Federal Plaza, 23rd floor, NY 10278."

"Mister Milano, are you in trouble? Do you need my help?" Roberts asked in a low voice.

"No, Sir," Jonny replied. "It's just something they have been wanting."

Hoping this would take Vallario off the street and no longer for him, Jonny felt a minute of relief. This might get rid of the price on his head, and people looking and searching every niche and corner for him. Relief lasted only a few minutes. "Damn! What if I'm wrong?" He ran his hand across the sweat on his forehead then paced the floor, considering the pros and cons of his actions. "The Mafia never forgets. Well, they'll find out neither do I. Taking the books out of play won't change anything. Vallario behind bars will be my payback for Carlene."

He realized that Duffy's Inn would not protect him forever. It would be just a matter of time before someone came there looking for him. With enough threats, Duffy would eventually have to point to room 323. His options were now limited; get the *job* done now or search for another *Duffy Inn* not so close to the city. All he had left to live for was revenge, and he would not let that be taken away from him. He decided to make a big jump to the southern border near where it all began, in Mexico.

CHAPTER 12

Jonny slept most of the four-hour flight from New York to El Paso. After putting his suitcase into the trunk of the first taxi he saw, the driver asked, "Where to?"

"I just need a motel that's not too expensive."

"Sure, I know a small place."

The ride to the motel was accompanied by never-ending chatter from the taxi driver that only stopped when he entered a dark street. "Here we are. Not much of a place to settle down in, but you asked for something cheap."

"I won't be here long, so this will do for now," Jonny said as he took his suitcase from the trunk then handed the driver a twenty-dollar bill. After the taxi left, he stood in front of the shabby building that made Duffy's Inn look like a mansion. While he was checking in, a long-legged woman came in. She nodded to him as she went to one of the three worn-out chairs in the lounge.

"Checking in or out?" she asked as she opened one of the tattered magazines next to her.

Jonny smiled. "Just checking in."

She pointed to the chair next to her. "Want some company?"

"I'm too tired for any company tonight but maybe later."

"I hope so. It's would be nice to talk to someone who speaks English for a change. My name's Maria."

"Maria! Like the restaurant Maria?"

She laughed and nodded. "Don't you know we're all named Maria? It's a law."

After reaching his room, Jonny tossed his suitcase across the bed. The bed responded with a deep sink, boasting of many years and many bodies having laid on it. After scanning the small room, he turned to the small window that overlooked a dark, narrow alley. As he looked into the darkness, he began wondering if he had made the right decision. It wasn't the sagging bed, the smudgy window, or the shallow scenery that concerned him; it was his failure to come up with a plan that would have any chance of success.

He started to challenge the bed and get some sleep. Then hunger overcame his fatigue. He was surprised to see a real telephone on a small table in the corner. Following the faded instructions, he dialed the front desk. After several rings, a coarse voice answered in Spanish. Jonny responded in the same language: "Where is the closest restaurant?"

"Depends on what you want," the desk clerk asked with one hand on the phone, the other or his girly magazine.

"I want a Mexican restaurant, one that is quiet and clean."

"Not likely here, but your girlfriend is still down here. She might know a place," the clerk said as he hung up and turned to the next page showing a young girl naked on a stool.

After a quick cold towel on his face, Jonny met Maria on the sunken lobby couch. "I thought you were anxious to get some sleep," she said as she waved at Jonny.

"Hunger got the best of me. The grumpy old guy there said you might know where I can find a good Mexican restaurant."

"That would be the Cabana. It's a cab drive away, but it's worth it . . . if you can afford it."

Jonny pulled his wallet out of his pocket, stared into it, then nodded. "I think I can cover it for one meal. You want to come with me?"

"Sure, if you're buying," she said with a wide grin.

She was right about the Cabana. It was quiet, clean, and expensive, something he had missed for a long time. After a heavy dinner, several glasses of bourbon while hearing Maria babble about the poor condition of this part of El Paso, they headed back to the motel.

⊰⊱ ◆ ◆ ⊰⊱

The sunlight forcing its way through the window woke him up. He looked out the window while rehearsing his plan. The sunlight revealed what the night had hidden: homeless men spread out like seals on ice, except the ice was tainted by years of dust and rust. He decided this would be as safe a place as anywhere. during his, hot water giving way to cold water then back again, shower, depending on who was flushing in another room, his thoughts turned to his new acquaintance.

He assumed Maria was in the *lady of pleasure* business. Surprised she didn't push herself on him during dinner, he figured she was new to the business or was either tired. Maybe she was in the *lady's monthly period*. Whatever the reason, he was glad she didn't. Someone to talk to was more important to him, and she was adept at that. It was at the dinner that the idea came to him.

Early the next morning he saw Maria sitting at a table on the sidewalk under a once multicolored parasol, coffee cup in one hand, a worn magazine in the other. As she waved at him, he waved back then he had a sudden thought: *Had it not been for Tucker stepping into Carlene's life, this could have been her. Maybe I can help this girl.* "Hello. Hope that's coffee and there's more of it somewhere."

"You're an early getter-goin' person, too," Maria said. "Your wish has come true, it is coffee. Sit down and I'll find you a cup." Minutes later, she returned with a steaming cup of coffee. "This is pretty strong stuff. Not that mild stuff they call coffee north of Texas."

"Thanks," Jonny said as he pulled up a chair. "I'd think this is kinda early for someone in your profession, but I welcome the company."

"*Profession?* Just what do you think my profession is?"

Jonny's face reddened. His speech was stuttered. "You know, *you want some company* type of profession."

Maria choked on the mouthful of coffee in her mouth, then laughed. "I don't know if I should be insulted or flattered, but--"

"I'm sorry. I just thought--"

Maria's choking from laughing with a mouthful of coffee cut Jonny off. As she wiped the drops of coffee running down her chin she said, "It's my fault. You seemed to be alone, it was early in the night, and you had a *I'm lost* look on your face. Well, not just that. It was more like, I needed company. As you can see, there aren't many people around here that speak English or have the same thought you came up with."

"Anyway, I apologize," Jonny said as he dabbed at a missed coffee drop with his hand. "You told me enough about this place last night. Let's start over. How long you been on this side of the border . . . There I go again assuming . . . but your accent and all."

"That's okay. I can change the looks, but can't get rid of the accent," she said with a shrug.

"That's a start," Jonny said as he smiled at her. But there must be more to you than the accent thing. So tell me more."

"Not much more to tell," Maria said with a sigh. "I grew up on the other side of the border. I didn't have much of an education. Hell, who on the other side of the border does. Even a college degree isn't enough when there aren't any jobs available. So I left Juarez a few years ago and came here hoping to find a better life . . . a legal life, I must add. I found work at the beauty parlor a few blocks from here. Even though it doesn't pay much, I get by. I like the work, and I learned a lot."

"Humm," Jonny said. "Sounds like you would like to have your own shop."

"Give it a little dignity, Sir. It's a *Parlor*, not a *Shop*! And it takes a lot to get one started. I tried to save over the years, but after a place to stay, food to eat, money sent to those I left behind, there hasn't been much left to save. So for now, it's just a dream."

"And . . . again I'm assuming," Jonny said, "you're staying in this *place*, too?"

Maria nodded. "Ya, at least for now. I keep looking for something better, but you have to settle with what you can afford." After another drink of coffee, she pointed to Jonny. "Okay, I've told you about my life, now tell me about yours."

Jonny waved his hand as if the wind would shift the conversation away from his life. "What little there is to tell is boring,"

"I bet it's more mystery than boring," she said with a smile. Then she pointed to the motel. "For example, you don't look like the type that would stay in a place like this just because it's cheap."

"You go where you go for different reasons," Jonny replied.

"And what was your reason?" After a pause without an answer, she shook her finger at Jonny. "I think your reason was that you got lost, hiding from someone--maybe the law, or running from an angry wife." When she didn't get a response, she shook her finger again. "But then, it could be because you are just cheap--cheap, but a friendly cheap."

"Ouch! I prefer to think of it as a convenience," Jonny said with a wide smile, a smile he seldom shared.

After an hour of conversation that went nowhere, Jonny turned the conversation back to her job. "You said you liked working in the beauty parlor. What if you didn't have to settle for just *getting by*. Maybe owning your own business ... in a better place?"

"It's like I said, it's just a dream."

"Maria, trust me," Jonny said with a wink. "I make dreams come true."

"I've heard that before," Maria said with a chuckle.

"Laugh now, young lady, but give me a day or two and you'll see."

"I'll try to get to bed early so I can pull up that dream," Maria said with a faked frown. "But now, I've got to go to work."

"You gotta have faith, young lady," Jonny said as he shook his head and gave her a mocking grin. "Anyway, I'll be here all day. Stop by after work and we can go to dinner. That is if you want to talk more about *dreamland*."

⊰ ◈ ◈ ⊱

The sun was setting when Jonny heard a knock on his door. Being cautious, he pulled his gun from out of his pillow. "Who is it?"

"It is me, the dreamer."

It took him a minute to recognize Maria's flippant voice. "Dreamer? That's what I was until someone banged on my door . . . just kidding." Then he grinned . . . *kidding* was not something the solemn Jonny Mirano ever did, until now. "Give me time to clean up and I'll meet you downstairs."

"Ya better hurry up, I'm bare naked and headed for the beach."

"What about the beach?"

Maria laughed. "So you're deaf after all."

"Maybe, but I can still see. So you better get some clothes on . . . just kidding."

He heard her laughing even louder as he started to shave. Looking into the mirror, he hesitated and repeated what he had just said, *Just Kidding*. It felt good.

Dinner consisted of tacos and cheap wine, both consumed under the washed-out parasol. "This is not quite what I had in mind," Jonny said after finishing off a glass of the bland wine. "I was planning on taking you back to another fine restaurant to impress you."

"Senor Milano," Maria said with a smile. "You impressed me when you first spoke to me."

Jonny blushed. Impressing someone was not in his vocabulary until now. Following the blush, his thoughts drifted away from Maria back to the only woman he ever loved . . . *It's okay, Carlene. She isn't a replacement; she's just a pawn in a chess game. Once I get to the King, the game will be over.* Then he returned to the present. "I was not kidding when I told you I could make your dream come true."

"There you go again with the Tooth Fairy thing," Maria said as she raised her upper lip. "See, I have all my teeth . . . where were you when I was losing them?"

With a sorrowful look, Jonny took her hand. "Okay, I'm sorry I wasn't there then . . . but I'm here now."

"You are forgiven," Maria said with a scrutinizing look. "Okay, back to the real world and your *magical* *proposition. . .*opps, I guess *magical* isn't part of the real world. Anyway, tell me what I need to do and what I get for doing it."

Jonny's sternness caught her attention. "You only have to be a good actress."

"I can do that, *Mister Butler.*" She replied with a southern accent.

Jonny shook his head. "Not bad, but this is not a *Gone with the Wind* movie, *Scarlett*. You just need to act like a greedy businesswoman, one that is not easily frightened. That should be all you have to do."

"Should be? That sounds like a mystery."

"Not really. I know what I want to do, just not sure how to do it. But I'll let you know the details once I figure everything out. As far as what you'll get . . . how about owning the beauty parlor you now work at?"

Maria shook her head. "I don't think she would sell it even if I had the money."

"Everything is for sale, Maria, if the price is right. But there are a lot of other places that might be even better," Jonny said with another of his newly found smile. Behind the smile, he was thinking about his priority, Garcia. His plan started with a telephone call then a flight back to NYC.

CHAPTER 13

G arcia was in his restaurant drinking his third glass of Cabrito Tequila when the other Cartel drug lords arrived. Their item of concern was Jonny Milano, the murder of Don De Luca, and the drain of money coming out of their pockets.

"Carlo, you made a big mistake in killing the gringos," Miguel said. "De Luca would have been easier to work with."

Garcia slammed his fist onto the table and glared at Miguel. "It's easy to criticize after the boat leaves the dock. Who would have thought one of their own would kill our *friend?* I can tell you, no one! Not you, or you, or you," he said as he pointed to each of the Capos. "So don't point your greasy fingers at me while drinking my tequila."

"Carlo is right," Morales said, as he turned to Miguel then back to Garcia. "That gringo Vallario and his imprudente socias are to blame. I think we need to meet with the Teniente's and tell them to send hit men to visit both of them."

"His associates might be reckless," Garcia said, "but they don't want a war any more than I do, but killing a gringo Don would start one. Eliminating gringo Milano would not be a problem. In fact, it would be a blessing to them." Everyone nodded. "Then, let's give this more thought and meet again next week. We'll find someway to deal with the Americanos. In the meantime, enjoy the tequila."

"Senor Garcia," the bartender whispered in his ear. "You have a phone call."

"Take a message and I'll call them back."

"Senor, he insisted to speak with you."

Garcia slapped his hand on the table again and looked up at the bartender. "Just who is so important that they can interrupt my meeting?"

"The gringo, Milano," the man said."

Garcia's eyes widened. "Jonny Milano?

Perhaps the sheep will come to the slaughterhouse," then he picked up the phone. "I'm surprised to hear from you, Señor Milano," he said softly. "What can I do for you?"

"More like what I can do for you, Senor Garcia."

"I hear you are no longer welcome in New York. So what makes you think we have anything more in common?"

"I believe we have the same goals in common, Señor, and I can help you obtain them."

"I do all right without gringos helping me, Señor."

"You are doing okay," Jonny said. "But I believe I can help you do a lot better."

"I hear your Don Vallario put a . . . what word, yes, a bounty on your head. Other than that, the only thing you could bring to me is an agreement that favors us. But, what is the Americano saying . . . *the train has left the station.*"

"Words travel fast, but just hear me out," Jonny said.

"Okay, Senor, tell me how you can help me."

"For one," Jonny said, "while Vallario is giving a one-time payment, I can give you recurrent payments as compensation. There will be a lot more pesos than the petty amount Vallario thinks I'm worth."

"It's not all about money, Señor Jonny. It's about honor . . . You have to pay for the murder of our *friend*, Senor De Luca."

"It's always about the money, Señor Garcia," Jonny said, again with another chuckle. "And Vallario is . . . was not your friend. Yes! He did warn you of Vallario's setup. But he did that only to get your trust so--"

Garcia cut Jonny off. "What could he gain by betraying the other Dons?"

"Just hear me out, Señor," Jonny said. "De Luca would have gained a lot. First, less competition if you retaliated by assassinating Vallario. Then, as being the only Don you would trust, he would step in and prevent an all-out war. Then he's the hero and one step higher to the top of the Mafia totem pole."

Garcia laughed. "So far what you tell me has little to do with business south of the border."

"I admit. Very little," Jonny said. "I am just trying to tell you why De Luca betrayed his para socios. Despite the apparent deadlock with business with you, he could change his position on accepting the higher cost of your *product* and seek other providers and focus on the Mafia's other income makers . . . loan sharking, gambling, longshoreman, unions . . . until you lower your prices. Again, another step-up."

"I still have no interest in your gringo's problems," Garcia said. "So tell me, why are you suddenly interested in our *business*."

"I've been neglected by my old boss too long, mainly because they see me as just a *businessman* instead of *one of them*. Well, they're right; I'm not only a businessman but a businessman who understands their *business* more than they do. For example, they think your prices are going up because of greed, but--"

"And why do you think prices go up?"

"It's simple. Your prices go up for the same reasons all businesses' prices fluctuate," Jonny said, then paused giving Garcia time to digest what he had said. "It's a matter of supply and demand. Getting your *product* over the border is getting harder and harder because the entry ports are getting more and more attention. Add to that, your tunnels are also getting closed. Less business means less profit. To make up for the lost money, you have to raise your price. The Dons don't understand that. I do."

"And what do you plan to do with all that business knowledge?"

"I want to use it to get into the game on my own. You can help me do that!'

"Ah. All of a sudden you're a greedy man . . . I like that, but tell me, what can you do for me?"

"I can solve your *distribution* problems."

"And how can you do that, Señor Jonny?" Garcia asked.

"I have contacts that others don't."

"Everyone says they have contacts. Why should I believe yours are any better than theirs?"

"Set up a meeting with me in Ciudad Juarez and I'll tell you."

"Okay, but come alone," Garcia said after a few minutes to access the benefit of a meeting. If none, he had Jonny in his hand. If there were benefits, it could mean pesos in his pocket. "Okay, Señor Jonny. We will meet where we met before."

"No! Not a hotel," Jonny said with a laugh. "Meeting in hotels and conference rooms haven't treated me well. How about a restaurant? I think we both will be more comfortable there."

Garcia laughed. "Ah, Senor, you have a sense of humor after all. I'll ease your concerns. There is a nice restaurant next door to the hotel called The Sonora Grill. We can meet there at five o'clock three days from now."

After Garcia hung up, Morales looked at him and shook his head. "Meeting him at the Grill? How do we deal with him in public and daylight?"

"Calm down, Morales. I know what I'm doing," Garcia said with a frown. "After the gringo feels comfortable and more trusting, we will take him to a more private place where we can put him to *rest*."

While Garcia was planning a way to kill Jonny, Jonny was planning a way to kill him. He had already found a way if he could convince Maria to help him.

It was a bright Monday morning when Jonny knocked on Maria's door. After several minutes, Maria opened the door. "Oh, it's you, Jonny," she said with a yawn then unlatched the door chain. She had a different look early in the morning with her hair disarranged, thick pale lips, a thin sagging gown, and drooping eyes. "Sorry about the look, but what do you expect this early in the morning?"

As Jonny looked at her, he realized this was the first time he had seen her without makeup and fancily dressed. Tall and slim, dark brown hair, with matching brown eyes--another Carlene but younger. "What I see, madam, is a young lady who wants a better life."

"You *coming on* to me?" she asked with a loud laugh. "You are really hard up, old man."

Being caught off guard he muttered, "Uhh, no, no. Nothing like that. You just remind me of someone I used to know."

She started to ask who but decided not to. Instead, she pointed to a well-worn couch then to the brewing coffee pot and said, "Well, help yourself to some coffee while I make myself look presentable."

Many minutes later, Maria returned. "Now, what made you bang on my door so early in the morning."

"I just wanted to let you know I'm going away for a day or two and tell you what I am going to do when I return and what I'm asking you to do."

"Oh, you mean the *movie star* part I need to play."

"Well, yes. But it's a lot more. Probably a lot more than you will want to be involved in."

After telling her about Mexico, what he was going to do, what he wanted her to do, and why, she looked wide-eyed at him. "You're asking a lot. Let me think about it while you're gone."

As Maria opened the door she. hugged him. The sudden hug was a happy surprise for Jonny. All he could think of was, "Remember what I told you, sometimes you have to do bad things to get good things."

An hour later Jonny was boarding a plane at El Paso International Airport and heading to Newark Liberty Airport in New Jersey. Four hours later he was in a taxi heading for South Broad Street. An hour and ten grand later, he left with a package, rented a car, and started a journey he had made before. However, this time the trip wasn't for him.

⬖ ✦ ⬗

Tucker's Tavern looked much the same. However, memories of a girl, beaches, and a friend were trampled by memories of the murder of his friend and the girl he loved.

"What do you think about it, Mister Milano?" the gray-haired agent asked.

"It's going to take a lot of work, Misses Collins. A lot of work."

"The price as a bar is well below its retail value. Guess that's because of the--"

"Yes, I heard about that. Anyway, I want it. If it's okay, I can transfer enough money to cover the property and the upgrade into your company's account by tomorrow. If any money is left over, give it to the new owner."

"Oh, this is not for you?"

"No, it's for my daughter. If there are any problems, she can take care of them." Jonny reached out his hand. "Guess you have a sell, Mrs. Collins." After the agent left, Jonny pulled out the picture of him and Carlene, the only picture he had of her. Old memories overtook him. *I wanted to buy your house, but it was repossessed. My fault. Sorry about that. Anyway, I bought this. Tell Tucker it's having a minor upgrade, but not to worry, Maria will take good care of it for her.*

After putting the past behind him, he took a cab to the airport, rented a private jet, and headed back to El Paso. Private flights did not require scanning your luggage.

Once he was back at his temporary home, he gently put his package under the bed. After a few hours of rest, he took a cab to a women's shop nearby and purchased a large shopping bag, high heel shoes, and a revealing black dress, then he looked at his watch; eight o'clock. "Maria should be home from work by now." After finding the courage, he knocked on her door. No answer. Frustrated, he started back to his room. Without Maria, he had no plan. When he heard footsteps coming up the steps, he took a deep breath.

"I see you're back from your business trip," Maria said with a wide smile as she unlocked the door. "Hope it went well."

"I think it did. At least I got a lot of things taken care of."

"What's in the bag?"

Jonny opened the bag revealing the black dress, shoes, and shopping bag. "If you decide *not* to go with me to Mexico, it's just a little token for you. If you have decided to go, then you can call it a costume. Either way, you get to keep the dress and shoes."

"I like it," Maria said as she held up the dress. "The shoes and the empty shopping bag, not so much. But they go well with the costume."

CHAPTER 14

When Maria saw the Cadillac Jonny rented for their brief trip to Juarez, she raised her eyebrows as she ran her finger over the soft leather. "Very snazzy, but it's appropriate for a classy gal like me."

Jonny waved a finger. "It's just for show, so don't get used to it." Then he took a deep breath and looked at her. "If you want to back out, do it now. I'll understand. But you need to tell me now."

"It's okay. I just keep telling myself you're the Puppet Master pulling all the strings and I'm the puppet."

"Just don't let the strings break, and remember, guys like Garcia are dangerous. It's *An Eye for an Eye*, so says the Bible. And remember, you don't know me, and be sure you remember your lines because you'll be on your own."

Maria nodded. "Practiced them while you were gone."

"The most important thing, Maria, is if it looks like things aren't going like the plan, get the hell out of there."

"Don't worry. I've got it. Hitchcock would be proud."

Jonny and Maria arrived at the Maria Chuchena restaurant half an hour before Garcia. While Jonny waited in the Cadillac, Maria went into the restaurant, looked around, then sat at one of the few empty tables. Jonny was waiting at the door when Garcia arrived with three of his men trailing behind him. "I thought this was to be a meeting between just the two of us. But it looks like you brought your entire family with you."

"Alone was meant for you, Señor Milano."

Once inside, Garcia ordered a bottle of Cabrito Tequila. While he was filling their glasses, Jonny was scanning the room. Maria was two tables away from him. A mother with a young girl and another child in a stroller children were sitting a table away. Seeing Jonny looking at them, she smiled and waved at him. Jonny returned her smile and returned to his survey of the room. Tourists were scattered around, most waiting for a table. It looked like Family Day. *Damn, too many people.*

Jonny tried to make eye contact with Maria chattering with a short, pungy young man wearing short pants, a short-sleeved T-shirt with "Dodger" stamped across it, and a cap turned around on his head. She was good at playing her role as a girl looking for fun.

Garcia noticed his interest. "Señor Jonny, you can entertain one of the pretty senoritas later, but for now, let us raise a toast to our new relationship." Jonny raised his glass in response. After the routine click of glass on glass, Garcia continued. "Now, tell me about your *contact.*"

"My contact is an employee at a beauty parlor in El Paso, who is eager to go from employee to owner." "And where do we come into the picture?"

Before Jonny could answer, Maria left the portly tourist and headed towards their table. "Hey, guys, can I join you," she asked as she put her shopping bag on the floor and sat down next to Garcia. Wide-eyed, she looked at Garcia. "Oh my God, I know you. You're that movie star, Felipe something. I saw your last movie, and it was great. Can I have your autograph?"

Garcia nodded to one of his guards who quickly lifted Maria out of her chair and pushed her toward the door. The shopping bag stayed under the table. As Maria stumbled out of the door, she shouted, "That's no way to treat your fans, Felipe whatever your name is. I'll never see another one of your movies again."

Jonny forced a laugh. "Didn't know you were a movie star, Señor Garcia, or whatever your stage name is." Grabbing the shopping bag and headed toward the door. "Seems your fan left her shopping bag." After a step, he was stopped by Garcia's guard. He tried to hide his fear with another laugh. "Don't worry, I'll be right back." After a nod from Garcia, the muscular guard stepped aside.

Once Jonny reached the door, he shouted, "Miss, you forgot something." That was Maria's signal that things were going downhill, and the backup plan was to be put into action. When Maria came back to the door, Jonny whispered, "Go back to El Paso and pack up all of your things. I'll meet you there."

Maria jerked the bag from his hand and glared at Garcia and the guard and shouted, "At least one of you know how to treat a woman."

Jonny gave her a devilish look. "Don't overdo it. Go now!"

Jonny found himself in a no-win situation. If he told Garcia more about Maria and the van, it wouldn't be difficult for him to track her down. If he didn't tell him now, he would end up in some cellar with Toro having fun beating the information out of him. Either way, Maria would no longer be a mystic woman, and Jonny B wouldn't be needed any longer. Neither of the options was acceptable. *Maybe there's a third option*, he asked himself. *I could feed him part of what he wanted to know. Holding back could buy him some time.*

Toro's sudden appearance interrupted his thoughts. "Now where were we before your fan interrupted us?" Jonny said as he reached the table.

"You were about to tell me about your contact until that estupido gringo got your attention," Garcia said.

Jonny winked as he sat down. "Stupid maybe, but very pretty. But back to our conversation. I know a woman who works in a beauty parlor on the other side of the border. She makes weekly runs across the border in the parlor's van. She's done this for so long, the border patrol no longer bothers to check her car or have dogs sniffing around it. She's a perfect solution to your problem . . . to *our* problem."

"Just where is this beauty parlor?" Garcia asked.

"Señor Garcia, we both know if I tell you that, you won't need me any longer. Then you would cut me out of the deal . . . or worse."

Garcia put his arm on Jonny's shoulder and squeezed it firmly. "You are right; I could let Toro take you somewhere quiet and ask the same questions. It would not take long before he got what I wanted."

"Yes, I know," Jonny said as he gently moved Garcia's arm from his shoulders. Not understanding the hostility in the movement, the drug lord opened his mouth just enough to show his crooked, stained teeth in what he considered a smile. "But I also know you are a wise businessman, and a wise businessman knows they don't always get everything they want. And being a wise businessman, you are willing to put revenge aside if you can benefit more than you give."

"Señor Garcia, I guarantee I can benefit you more alive than dead."

"How would you do that, Jonny B?"

Jonny smiled as he ignored the question. "What happened to *Señor* Jonny?"

"Jonny B is less formal," Garcia said as his thick hand was back on Jonny's shoulder. "And I think we should be less formal if we are going to work together, don't you?"

Jonny nodded. "I prefer it that way."

"Ah, see, we are already coming to agreements." After refilling his glass, he shook his head, in a motion of false confusion. "Still, how can you assure me that I won't lose my *product* at the border?"

"To show my loyalty and to remove that concern, I'll bring the lady here in a couple of days. Then you can send her across the border with a small package of the *product*. One of your men can follow her to make sure she crosses without any difficulty. That should put you more at ease."

Garcia leaned back in his chair, ran his hand across his face then nodded. "You understand that if she is stopped, it is on you?"

"Of course. I would not want it any other way, my *friend.*"

"Our business here is finished . . . for now," Garcia said as he finished his tequila and motioned to the bearish looking man standing against the wall. "Toro, I'm going to the car. You can set this up with our friend, Jonny."

Toro looked every bit like the bull he was named after, but somehow, he managed to squeeze his thick body into a chair next to Jonny. Narrow, dark eyes glared at Jonny as the Mexican gave him instructions with his limited English. "I meet contact and van here, four o'clock Thursday," he said as his sweaty hand slapped a handwritten map on the table. "If nobody show up after fifteen-minutes, you and your girl are fair game." Then he stood up and looked down at me with a grizzly grin and said, "I hope nobody show up."

Thursday came, but Jonny did not.

⬥ ⬥ ⬥

While Garcia was taking out his wrath on Toro, Jonny was helping Maria pack the rest of her clothes. As he closed her suitcase, he slipped back into his past: *Another Carlene . . . another life I might destroy.* Not sure what to do, he put his arms around her, not a lover's hug, but a hug a father would give his daughter leaving for college. "I'm sorry for putting you through all of this, Maria, but--"

"No apologies, no buts. I knew the risk I was taking. Besides, I've been wanting to leave this town for years. Now I get to leave . . . and in a black Cadillac, even if it's only to the airport. That's more than I ever thought I would be in . . . except for my funeral."

"There are a lot of Cadillacs where we're going."

"And just where are we going? I want to know . . . I need to know."

"A nice place. I promise you'll like it. I'll make sure you do. Other than that, it's a surprise."

◈ ◈ ◈

After six hours on a Delta jet, Jonny and Maria were in another rented black Cadillac going towards Havens Beach. During the two-hour drive, Maria pestered Jonny by singing along with the radio's country songs. The annoyance was only broken with demands to know where they were going and how long would it take to get there.

"I hope you're a better *shampooist* than you are a singer," Jonny said after an hour of musical torture. Although country music was not his style, he liked hearing Maria sing, even if she was off-key at times. This was a new change in Jonny Milano, the accountant. Jousting had never been in his vocabulary. His grin showed he liked it.

"I'll have you know, Mister Know-It-All, I'm a cosmetologist not a, whatever you said, and I'll stop singing when you tell me where we're going."

"We'll be there soon. I think I can endure your punishment a little longer."

Ten minutes later, Jonny was parking in front of Tucker's Tavern. Seeing a dozen men grinding, cutting, hammering, measuring, taking things out, and putting other things in, Maria gave Jonny a pouting look. "A bar? We're going to a bar? A bar that's being torn apart and put back again?"

Jonny responded by shrugging his shoulders followed by a wide grin. "I'm not sure this--"

Before he could finish his false response, a bearded man holding a layout of floor plans for up and downstairs interrupted him. "You the new owners?"

Jonny shook his head. "This young lady is the new owner. But you can show both of us the layout you plan."

Maria gave the architect a befuddled look, then back at Jonny. "A bar, Jonny. I own a bar. You gotta be kidding; I don't know anything about bar business or whatever you call it."

Jonny choked back a laugh. "Right now it's a bar . . . or now a piece of a bar, but when this gentleman and his crew finish, you will have your own beauty parlor downstairs and a very nice apartment over it."

While trying to hold back her tears, Marie looked at the two-story building again, then back at Jonny. "I don't know what to say. If this is a joke, Jonny Milano, you will pay heavily for it."

"I don't know what you guys are talking about," the architect said as he pointed to several computer design sketches, "but I need you to look at this design. It's just like you asked--upgrading the upstairs apartment and building a beauty parlor downstairs."

"A *beautiful* beauty parlor downstairs," Jonny reminded the bearded man.

Tears in her eyes, Maria wrapped her arms around Jonny. "My own business? My own business?" Then she took a deep breath. "There goes my Cadillac."

Jonny laughed. "That will be here tomorrow, my lady."

"Oh my God," Maria said as she wiped the tears running down her cheek. Then she narrowed her eyes. "Black?"

"Of course," Jonny said.

After the architect showed her the reconstructing plans, She and Jonny went to a nearby hotel. "I hope this place suits you until your new apartment is finished. It's close enough to the construction for you to drop by whenever you want to see how it is going. I'm going to open a bank account in your name so you have enough money to live on until you are back in business and have a steady income."

Before Maria could answer, Jonny put his finger over her closed mouth. "Hush! It didn't go as I wanted it to, but you put your life on the line for me. All of this is not enough to repay you."

"You will be here to help me, won't you?"

"You don't need me. Besides, I've got other business to take care of elsewhere."

Tears ran down Maria's cheeks as she laid her head on Jonny's shoulder. "Can't you come back once you do whatever you have to?"

Jonny gently pushed her away, wiped the tears away with his fingers, and shook his head. "I would just put you in danger. I did that to another girl, and I won't do it again. But I won't forget you."

"When are you leaving?"

"When the sun rises tomorrow."

Face now in her cupped hands. "Will you stay with me tonight?"

"Only if I can sleep on the couch."

Tears again. "But--"

"No *buts* and no more tears. You're more like a daughter to me than a girlfriend." He lifted her face and smiled. "And what I need now, more than anything else, is a family."

Sunrise was an hour away when Jonny quietly kissed Maria on her forehead. When she woke, Jonny was gone. She looked out the window to see if he was outside. He was not. Then she saw the note on the table:

If you have an emergency, you can reach me at this number, but only if it's an emergency. By the way, your Cadillac should arrive today. Drive carefully. Love you . . . I don't say that often, but I'm beginning to like it. Jonny

CHAPTER 15

The cab dropped Jonny off at the same auto dealership that was taking Maria's new car to her. "Guess, I'll be out of business, Mister Jones, now that you're buying a new car," the cab driver said with a laugh as he handed Jonny his small suitcase."

"Sorry about that, Bobby, but you and the airport are putting me in the poor house. Anyway, I think you'll survive," Jonny said as he handed the driver his fee and a healthy tip. "This should put food on your table for a while."

As the cabby drove away, Jonny looked back towards the east where he had so many memories. He tried to push away the bad memories and focus on the good ones: Evenings listening to Tucker's chatter and occasional complaint about nothing as he cleaned glasses, sandy beach walks, days and nights with Carlene, seeing Maria's tears of happiness when she looked at her shop to be. It wasn't long before a sudden downfall of rain brought him back to the present and sending him running into the dealership.

After a complimentary cup of coffee, the salesman who sold him Maria's Cadillac insisted that, now that he was a *faithful* customer, he could buy another Cadillac at a better price.

"I'm not as rich as you seem to think I am," Jonny said. "The Caddy was for my daughter. She always wanted one, and since it was her birthday, I splurged." Then he walked to the showroom window and pointed to an eight-year-old Ford on the lot. "That's what I need."

The Ford blended in his appearance to be on the downside of penniless as well as being inconspicuous. After eight hours on the road with three more days to go, he regretted not having the comfort of the Cadillac. Added to this, was three days in various, low-cost, motels. The only upside of the trip was the sleepless nights that gave him more time to plan on how to reach Garcia again. Everything he came up with had downsides, downsides like being killed. As he entered the outskirts of El Paso, his thoughts about the Cadillac turned into a plan.

Another night in a motel, this one more pleasant and more to his liking, he went over his plan, picking it apart with dozens of *what-ifs* and *how-tos*. Finally, he decided it would work . . . could work. Then he shook his head, *"Why didn't I think of this while I was in New York? Guess I'll have to go shopping."*

In New York, his purchases, even in the small amounts he needed, would cause a few raised eyebrows and a lot of questions. However, they seemed to be common purchases in El Paso, especially by the farmers. Next came a couple of phone calls. The first was to the bank, the other to Garcia, then a visit to the local Cadillac dealership.

"Henry," Jonny said in an as innocent tone as he could, "Mister Vallario wants to transfer another two-hundred-thousand into his grandkid's account."

Jonny was relieved when Henry didn't seem to know about the *changes* in Vallario's business arrangements. "It didn't take long for them to go through the first deposit, but that's what most spoiled rich kids do."

"I wouldn't know, Mister Milano. But there was a concern with that first deposit you put into this account. Mister Vallario called me about it. He sounded angry but said he would take care of it."

"Ya, I know. Mister Vallario wasn't angry with us, but he raised hell with the kids. Anyway, we resolved it, and I'm sorry he called you."

"So what is this deposit for?"

"The kids are going to college soon. One at Standford the other at Bard. I guess good old granddad wants to make sure they have enough in their accounts to pay for tuition and such. But there's a deadline for paying it, and--"

"I understand, Mister Milano, but I would appreciate it if you could come by the bank and sign off on this . . . just to keep me out of trouble?"

"Sure, Henry, I can do that, but I'm out of town right now."

"Can the deposit wait until you get back?"

"I guess so, but if it doesn't get there in time, the kids might have to wait for another semester. I don't think granddad would be happy about that. But, you can with check with him if you--"

"No, Mister Milano. Bothering Mister Vallario won't be necessary. Just tell him Henry at the bank said hello and good luck to his grandkids."

"I suspect Mister Vallario will be calling you in a few days. Then you can tell him yourself."

After hanging up, Jonny took a breath of relief. However, his relief was short. He knew the next person he had to call would not be as accommodating as Henry.

⟶ ◆ ◆ ⟵

Garcia was just getting to bed when his phone ring. Most calls on his phone were either from his wife complaining about not having enough money or an urgent call from one of his dealers complaining about a business problem. Since Mrs. Garcia was somewhere in Hawai spending his money, it had to be a serious *business* problem. However, this call was not about either.

"What's the problem now?" he shouted into the phone.

"No problem, Mister Garcia. At least not at this end."

Garcia didn't recognize the voice. "Who is this? How did you get this number?"

"As the negotiator between you and the New York Dons, I have all of your numbers."

"Jonny Milano! You must be neck-deep in shit to call me after the . . . what is the gringo word . . . the *scam* you pulled on me. Is your life only worth a few U.S. dollars?"

"I assure you, Señor Don, that was not a scam. My intentions were honest, but a lot of things went wrong. I want to explain them to you, but not over the phone. Can we meet again?"

"Señor Jonny, I'm not sure if you're a stupid man or a very brave man. It's rarely that a man would be damned and blessed at the same time. So tell me, are you brave or just stupid?"

"I would like to show you that I'm not either one. If anything, I like to think of myself as a *trusting* person. So, I'm trusting that you will hear me out if we meet."

"You may think of your self as being a trusting man, but I assure you, I am a cautious man . . . and an unforgiving man."

"Just a brief meeting. That's all I'm asking for."

Garcia went into a long, deep, laugh. "You risk your life for a brief meeting?"

"I'm asking for another meeting because I want to let you know why I didn't come back that day," Jonny said in a submissive tone. "I believe you are also a *fair man*, so--"

Before Jonny could finish, Garcia said, "Call me back in five minutes."

Five minutes later, Jonny dialed Garcia again, but it wasn't Garcia who answered. "Mister Milano, I will meet you tomorrow at--"

Jonny cut him off saying, "I need to speak to Señor Garcia, not one of his henchmen."

"I'm not *one of his henchmen* . . . I'm his son, Riccardo."

"Son or not, I want Señor Garcia on the phone and at the meeting."

"Wait a minute."

Jonny could hear jabbering in the background, then Riccardo was back on the phone. "He will be there. Ten o'clock sharp."

"At the same restaurant?" Jonny asked.

"No. At the same hotel conference room. You know, the one where you met the last time."

"He knows the last meeting there didn't go too well," Jonny said as memories of the *last time* brought back the helplessness, heavy breathing, gunshots, blood spurting, bodies falling on the floor, one of which was the body of a friend.

"He said there or no meeting at all."

Jonny fought back his anger. "I'll be there."

⬥ ⬥ ⬥

Jonny put together the items he recently purchased, connected a spring to part of the briefcase. Once he was certain that the spring would stretch once the briefcase was opened, he connected the other end of the spring to the package. Once he was satisfied that his contraption would work, he left the motel certain that Garcia would pay for killing Linny.

Next on his list was a visit to the nearest Cadillac dealership. After listening to another salesman's pitch, he left the Ford there and drove to S. El Passo Street into Juarez in a new, eight-cylinder, Cadillac Fleetwood. From there, he headed to the hotel conference room. Although the traffic was light, the memories of the past remained heavy.

He arrived at the hotel in the Cadillac ten minutes early; Garcia arrived ten minutes later in a black SUV. They parked close enough that he could see him and two other men.

The driver was the first to get out. He had tangled hair and clothes that matched his shabby beard. The other was years younger and taller, with a shaved face and clean clothes. Once he saw that Jonny was alone, the younger man motioned to Garcia and the seedy-looking man.

Getting out of the van, Garcia, dressed in his standard black suit, black shirt, and red tie, waved at Jonny. "Sorry I'm a bit late, Señor Jonny," he said as he approached. "But I'm here now. What do you have to say that is so important?"

"I'm hoping we can get past the last meeting. I know what happened was Don Vallario's doings, not yours. You had no choice. If I had been in your shoes, I would have done the same thing."

Garcia didn't respond. Instead, he and his son walked up to the Cadillac. "Fine ride you have here," the boy said as he ran his hand across the hood. "A very fine ride."

"You must be doing pretty good on your own," Garcia said as he opened the door and ran his hand over the Cadillac's leather."

"Not really. I need a job. I was hoping you could find me one."

"Why would he do that?" the boy said.

"Señor Garcia, I came here to negotiate with you, not this boy."

Riccardo stepped towards Jonny, looked eye to eye with him, and was about to say something when Garcia pulled him back. "The *boy* is my son, Riccardo. The idiot with him is Raul. Riccardo often forgets his place, but he's smart. He reminded me that since your Don is looking for you, bringing you to him alive or dead would go a long way in settling our differences."

"Maybe. But the Dons might see it as an opportunity to get you out of the way. Then they could negotiate with your local competitors."

"Let's get on with--"

Garcia cut his son off short. "Show some courtesy and don't speak until I tell you to speak." Then he smiled at Jonny. "Forgive the boy. He's spoiled . . . all his mother's fault. But he is right. We need to do what we came here to do."

The look on his son's face told him they were not here to negotiate. "Señor Garcia, I drove here in this Cadillac. It was to be a present . . . a peace offering. Why not just take these keys and let me walk back across the border?"

"I wish I could do that, Señor Jonny. I come to like you . . . but letting you off that easy would send a strong message to everyone that I was getting weak. I can't let that happen." Then he held out his hand. "But I will take the offer of the keys." Bouncing the keys in his hand, he turned to his son. "While I'm taking this beautiful car for a ride, you can give Señor Jonny a ride in the SUV."

Jonny didn't need to say anything. The grin on Riccardo's face was all that had to be said.

CHAPTER 16

Once they were deep into the Chihuahuan Desert, Riccardo pulled Jonny out of the black SUV. With his hands tied behind him, clothes soaked with sweat, and a painful dry throat, Jonny fell facedown into the hot sand. A booted foot in his side sent him onto his back. Although he could hear coyote cries in the distance, reminding them that this was their domain, the sun blinded everything except miles of sand and the Sierra Madre mountains in the west. As his sight improved, he saw scattered cactus, some tall thin plants, a rattlesnake curling up behind the front wheels of the van to get away from the burning sun, and two men in front of him. Suddenly, two strong arms pulled him to his feet, bringing more pain into his broken ribs.

"Stand up like a man," Raul said with a menacing frown.

Jonny staggered then dropped to his knees again. "If you're going to kill me, at least make it fast."

Riccardo laughed. "Jonny, Jonny, do you think we brought you here just to kill you? Hell, man, we could have done that miles back." Another kick followed, sending Jonny back into the baking sand. "My father might have made it clear you weren't to be hurt, but my man here just had to have some self-serving gratifications. I'll make him apologize if you like."

Loud laughter from Raul. "Mister Milano, I got out of hand. I am very sorry for that. Please forgive me."

Riccardo landed another kick to Jonny's side, laughed then said, "Cut his hands loose."

Raul looked confused. "But--"

"Just do what I said or I'll leave your skinny ass out here with him."

Despite his irritation with Riccardo's insults, Raul untied Jonny then jerked him back onto his feet. It took several minutes for Jonny to regain his balance. When he did, Jonny wiped away the sand blending with the sweat on his face. "What are you going to do?" he asked. "Let me bake in the sun while you watch?"

"Jonny, I'm insulted that you think I'm that bad. But we are going to play a game. You do like games don't you?"

"I'm not much for games."

"I think you'll like this one. Raul, I'm thirsty. Get the canteen out of the van."

Grumbling, Raul tossed him the metal canteen from the van. "Damn it, Riccardo, you're not going to give him a drink are you? Let's just do what we came here to do and get the hell back to civilization."

Riccardo took a deep drink, wipe his lips, then poured the rest of the water into the sand. "Okay, Jonny, the game now starts. No one has water, not me, not the idiot over there, not you. The goal of the game is to see who gets back to Juarez first, me and the idiot or you. The only advantage we have is that we're going back in an air-conditioned van and you . . . well, you have to walk."

Jonny picked up the empty canteen and walked towards Riccardo, shaking his head and waving the canteen. "Come on, Riccardo, it's miles from anywhere. Walking in this heat and in hot sand, there's no way I can survive without water. At least fill this--" Before Riccardo could respond, the canteen came down on his head. A strong fist followed on his chin sending him to the ground.

Gun in his hand, Raul ran towards Jonny. As he closed in, a size twelve boot hit him in the crotch. The groaning man bent in pain. Having the advantage, Jonny grabbed the gun lying in the sand and hit him on the side of his head with it. Turning back to Riccardo, he waved the gun. "I'll play your game, but with a slight change in the rules . . . you walk--I ride. Hand me the keys."

As he started the van, he saw another canteen full of water. "I thought you would be smart enough to have more than one." After a long drink, he tossed the canteen to the stunned man. "Take this, Riccardo. You're gonna need it more than me."

"You son of a bitch," Riccardo yelled as he grabbed the spilling canteen. "You're gonna pay for this when I get back."

"I don't think so, but when I see your dad, I'll tell him you might not be back for a while."

As Jonny arrived at the Paso del Norte Bridge pedestrian crossing, he had a brief feeling of resentment about leaving two men in the desert. It didn't take long for reality to overcome resentment. *Hell, if I hadn't left them, I would be the one shivering in the desert's nighttime cold. Worst, I would be the one freezing and panicking at the sound of coyotes and the bite of a disturbed rattlesnake.*

After parking the SUV on the Mexican side of the bridge's pedestrian crossing, he pushed his way through the crowd of tourists buying souvenirs and taking pictures. It didn't take long before an old man selling a variety of collectibles, water, and snacks, approached him. "Good water, good food, Señor, and very cheap."

"I'm short on money right now," Jonny said as he looked back at the parked SUV. "Tell you what. I'll trade that van over there for a bottle of water and two of your tacos."

The Mexican handed Jonny water and tacos. "You don't need to sell your car, Señor. You pay next time you cross over."

"I don't think I'll cross the bridge again, at least not for a while," Jonny said as he handed the man the SUV's keys. "Besides, I will have problems bringing it across to the other side."

"Problems?"

"You know . . . problems with the border patrol, like not having a license and all. If you have a cell phone I can use to make a call, we'll be even."

The bargain made, Jonny made his call. "Señor Garcia, this is your--"

"I know who you are. What I don't know is where you are. More important to me is where is my son?"

"The last time I saw him and his buddy, they were on their way home. Having to walk might have delayed them. But if you follow the tire tracks, you should run into them, that is if they make it at all."

"The game is over, Milano. As we speak, you are dead."

"Maybe, but I might have something that will give me your forgiveness." A long pause followed. "There's a briefcase in the trunk of the Caddilac. Inside it is a copy of Don Vallario's *business* ventures. If you have this in your hands, you have Vallario in your pocket."

"Very interesting, Señor, but my son is worth more than anything you can give me. But I wonder why you are giving me this *gift* when you know you are still at the top of my list of *problems*."

"Why? It's simple. Someone has to pay for murdering my friend, Linny. I can't get to you, but you can get to Vallario. Just open the briefcase and my debt to my friend is paid. I'll wait while you go to the car."

Jonny heard doors slamming, wind blowing, car trunk opening, then a deafening explosion. "Debt paid," he muttered as he handed the cell phone back to its owner. Then he walked the twenty minutes into El Paso and took what he hoped would be his last taxi ride.

CHAPTER 17

Vallario was in dilemma when he heard about Garcia. On one hand, he was no longer a problem. On the other hand, if Jonny was behind it, he might have become an even bigger problem. There was only one solution.

Vallario's meeting with Ferrari was short and to the point. "One of Milano's few friends was killed during a *business visit* in Mexico," Vallario explained. "Now, he's out to get revenge. I didn't think he had it in him, but the son of a bitch surprised me. If he could take out one Don and one of the Mexican Cartel, he won't think twice to put me . . . us . . . on his *to-do list.*"

"Lonzo, he was one of yours. That makes it your problem, so it is up to you to make sure your problem doesn't become my problem or problems for the other Dons. Find him!"

When the brief meeting was over, Vallario shook his head. There were only two answers, increase the bounty on Jonny's head and bring in someone who might have a clue about where Jonny might be. He called Paulie.

Vallario wasn't the only one worried, so was Paulie when he was summoned to Vallario's house. That was never a good sign . . . people called there often never came back.

Vallario's driver picked him up early the next morning. Once at Vallario's country mansion, he was met by Danny Veneto and another man he didn't know. The unknown grabbed Paulie by the arm and patted him down, something he had never gone through before. This only added to his anxiety."

"Come on, Danny," Paulie said as he raised his hands. "It's me, Paulie. Don Vallario is expecting me."

"Sorry, Paulie, but since what happened in Mexico, the *Man* don't trust nobody."

"He's not packing," the other guard said.

"I knew you would be clean," Danny said. "I'll take you to the boss. Topolino, you keep your eyes open out here while I take Paulie inside."

"I told you not to call me that," the other guard grunted. "I'm not a *little mouse.*"

Danny laughed. "Then stop sneaking around like one."

During the hundred-foot-path walk from the gate to Vallario's doorway, Paulie chatted with Danny, trying to get a clue as to why he was there. Danny only shook his head, "A lot of shit is going on since that bastard Garcia got blown up. You can thank your friend, Milano for that."

Vallario was pacing the floor when Paulie arrived. "Thanks for coming, Paulie," he said as he pointing to a chair. "I know you and Jonny were friends."

"I guess you could say we were friends, but then, he was friends with most people."

"But not as close as you. Anyway, friendship stops at the *office* door. I know you know that. That's why I called you." After lighting a cigar, he sat down at his desk. "You know he killed Garcia don't you?"

"That's what I hear, but I--"

Vallario raised his hand to cut Paulie off. "We need to find him. He must have left some footprints. I want you to find them. Then I want you to make sure he doesn't create any more problems for us."

"Boss, I'm not good at doing these types of things. Maybe you should send some of the other guys."

"It's time for you to become more involved, Paulie. Just remember, Milano isn't a Czar or even a hitman. He's just an accountant."

"Do you know his background?"

Vallario shook his head then gave the closed smirk he thought was a smile. "I know enough about him. His father asked me to give him a job after he left the Navy. He had only two years of college, not enough to get a degree, but he's smart, and he knows enough to keep up with the money that comes in and where to put it so no one can question it."

"He might be a good accountant, Boss, but there's a lot more to him than that." He was right, but very few knew about Jonny Milano's history.

⊷ ◆ ◆ ⊶

When Jonny Milano joined the Navy it didn't take him long to go from boot camp to Navy Seal. After four years wading in swamps and grueling training, he decided not to reenlist. Instead, he enrolled in a local college to become an accountant. At a New Year's Party in San Diego, his life changed again.

The lights were low in a large living room filled with loud people patiently waiting for the ball to fall, bringing in a new year. Jasen, the host and a long-time friend of Jonny, asked him to play bartender.

Jonny shook his head. "Jasen, I have a hard time making something as easy as a Bloody Mary."

"A Bloody Mary isn't all that easy," Jasen said with a pat on Jonny's back. "Just fake it, and give everyone straight bourbon or play it by ear. After a few drinks, no one will care."

Midway into the party, three men and a woman showed up. All four of them already had a drink too many. One of the men, short but muscular, pointed to a vacant chair and pushed the woman into it. Then he and the other two men found seats at the end of the bar. Short and muscular lit a cigarette and banged his fist on the table. "How 'bout a Bloody Mary for the lady over there, and a Boston Sour for me and my friends."

"I can make a Whiskey Sour if you'll take it without the egg, and I'll do the best I can with the Bloody--"

"Hell, man! What kind of a bartender are you? It's not a Boston without the egg white."

"I guess I'm not a very smart bartender," Jonny said with a forced smile. "But let me see if I can crack open an egg."

"Screw you!, Just forget the egg and make anything that has whiskey in it . . . and make it a double." Then he looked back at his wife. She was still in the chair talking with the hostess of the party. "See that beautiful girl over there? Bet you would like to have a piece of that. Too bad, Mister Blue Eyes, she's my wife." After another sneer, he picked up his drink and wobbled towards the beautiful, underdressed woman. When he reached her, she muttered something in his ear. The sneer on his face made it clear to Jasen's wife that the intoxicated man was angry. She was quick to get between the man and the woman. "I don't believe I know you," she said.

"No, Ma'am. I don't think we ever met," the man replied, now with a Cheshire Cat grin. "I'm Walter, but they call me Tank. The short guy over there is my brother, Eddy. That other guy is Tex, but we just call him Cowboy."

"Another brother?" she asked.

"No mam, he's just a friend."

After looking at the three men, she realized they were troublemakers. "And we know you from where?"

"We know your husband. He probably forgot to tell you we were coming." Looking down at the woman again, he patted her shoulder. "This is my wife, Kathy. I was just telling her not to drink too much because she's our driver tonight." He continued the smug grin. "I was just bringing her a drink." After a few babbling minutes, he pointed to Jonny who was still wiping up the spilled drink Tank knocked over when he left the bar. "Your bartender doesn't know much about mixing a simple drink. If you want, I'll relieve the jerk."

"That jerk happens to be a Navy Seal."

"A Seal, huh? Well, Happy New Year early." Then he worked his way back to the bar, giving everyone he passed a Happy New Year's greeting.

Once he was back at the bar, he sneered at Jonny. "Where did you get those pussy eyes?"

"Just came with the package, I guess."

"Just give me another drink, smart ass!"

"I think you've had enough already."

Fist hitting the bar again, "Being a Navy Seal, you must think you're pretty tough. But you don't--"

"That's ex-Navy Seal."

"Let's go outside, and I'll show you what tough is."

Jonny raised his hand as if in surrender. "Mister . . . whatever your name is, I don't want to fight you, but--"

Before Jonny could finish, the table Walter hammered his fist on the counter, then grabbed Jonny by the shirt collar, and pulled him away from the bar, then shouted to his two companions. "Eddy, you and Cowboy back my play."

It took Jonny only a minute before Eddy and Cowbow were laying on the floor moaning in pain, while Tank was wallowing in his own blood. Next to him was a broken bottle. Tanks' wife pushed Jonny away, shouting, "You cut him with a broken bottle . . . you tried to kill him."

Jonny left in handcuffs. After a brief trial, he was sentenced to six months in jail. Ninety days later, he was released with two years' probation. Although he didn't complete college, he had learned enough to do the basics, especially the basics of Forensic Accounting. Still, his past kept him from finding a professional job until his father introduced him to Alonzo Vallario. Vallario saw his past as a plus instead of a negative. Thanks to his father, he was hired by Alonzo Vallario.

Despite not completing college, he had learned enough to do the basics, especially the basics of Forensic Accounting. Thanks to his father, he was hired by Alonzo Vallario.

⬧⬧

Vallario's look sent a chill down Paulie's back. "So you're saying my *timid* accountant isn't as timid as he pretends to be."

"Yes. Even if someone found him, likely, we would never see that person again."

"That's all the more reason to send someone he thinks he can trust. That someone is you." Another scowling look. "Paulie, you need to decide whose side you're on."

Paulie nodded. "I'm on the *business's* side."

"I thought you would be. I promise I won't forget you. You can start with calling some of the Cartels across the border. Maybe they know something. Let them know that killing Garcia was not on us. We're looking for the rouge who did it, too. They might not talk to you, but it's worth a try. Just keep me informed."

Paulie left knowing what he had to do, a lot to do.

CHAPTER 18

Leaving Maria was hard, but Jonny knew he was right. Someone would soon track her down like they did Carlene. He had to leave New York and find a life somewhere else if Maria was to have a life. Back in his Ford, with his only suitcase, and what money he had left, he drove north towards Chicago. It didn't take him long to realize he was headed to a city just as bad as New York City. "Jesus, the homes of Capone, Nitti, and Ricca," he said. Then he turned south. Eight hours later he was just a few miles away from the Ohio border.

Fatigue and hunger made him pull into a rest area filled with tired truck drivers and a half-dozen cars. Under a full moon, he parked beside a Chevy and headed for the vending machines. After feeding them quarters he had several packages of Cheez-It crackers, two Snicker bars, and a paper cup of coffee. On the way back to his car the Chevy's license plate caught his eye. "Maybe a message from God," he said with a chuckle. After satisfying his hunger, he rolled down the car's window to get more fresh air than the cooped up Ford had allowed. He was about to sit back and get some sleep when he saw an elderly man and a woman walking back towards where he was parked. The woman appeared to be in her early fifties, the man looked a few years older. Both were dressed casually, the man in jeans, a dark tee-shirt under a light jacket, and a hat, the woman in a knee-high blue dress, and carrying a heavy purse over one shoulder. Jonny got out of the car and waited to see if the Chevy was theirs. It was.

"That your car with the Kentucky plate?" Jonny asked.

The man walked over to Jonny and smiled. "Yep, she's mine. A bit beat up but she still runs okay."

"I have to say the same thing about my Ford here. I notice the blue on white Kentucky plate. What part of Kentucky are you from?"

"West Port, not to be confused with that big Army school. Bet you never heard of it though. The population's only about three-hundred or so."

The woman joined the sudden conversation. "It's small but it has a lot of history. What about you?"

"I'm aware of your West Port and its military history. As for me, I'm from New York, but I'm leaving the big city. Too crowded and too expensive to live there anymore, so I decided to go down south. Kentucky was on my list of places. That's why I noticed your tag."

The man took off his Kentucky Wildcats cap, revealing his early balding. "Well, our city . . . I guess you Yankees would call it a town, might be just what you're looking for." Laughing, he continued. "Ya might need to get rid of that accent though."

"Hush, Waylon," the wife said as she pushed against her husband. "His accent's no more different than yours was to those in Ohio."

"I wasn't being rude to the man, Helen. Just joking." Then he shook Jonny's hand. My name's Roger, Roger Waylon. This is my wife, Helen. We went to Ohio to visit kids. Couldn't stay long because of business issues."

"My name's . . ." Jonny hesitated. He wasn't sure what name he was going to use. He decided on the name of an old Navy friend. "John . . . John Randell, but everybody calls me Jim."

"Well, Jim, it was nice talking to you. If you ever come to West Port stop by and see us. I work at the military museum. We're easy to find. You been in the military?"

"A few years in the Navy, but I'm a military history fan."

"Then you would love our little town. I can show you things that most people don't even know exist."

"Now, Waylon, don't get going with that history stuff. We have another ten hours or more if you want to get home." Then she turned to Jonny. "He'll bore you to death with all that stuff, Mister Randell."

"It's okay. Right now, I'm not sure where I'll end up, but Mister Waylon got my interest."

"No Mister, no Roger. Just call me Waylon. Everybody does. Somehow, no one seems to know I have a first name. I prefer Waylon anyway."

After the harsh years around Vallario and his people, Jonny found the Waylon family very refreshing. "Well, Waylon, don't be surprised if I show up at your doorstep."

⬤⬤⬤⬤ ✦✦ ⬤⬤⬤⬤

After several hours of deep sleep, Jonny was back on the highway. While driving, he thought about all he had left behind him, both the good and the bad.

Kill him? Not likely over a few grand.

Pay the Greek a visit.

The boss should just write off the debt.

Nicky doesn't have the money, and he can't get the money. It always boils down to money.

Fate or mistake, does it really matter? The outcome is the same.

Those blue eyes just begged a nickname.

Smile, Jonny B, the camera is watching.

Why would four men with guns be with you?

Don't you know we're all named Maria? It's a law.

I hope you're a better shampooist than you are a singer.

Mister Know-It-All, I'm a cosmetologist . . . I'll stop singing when you tell me where we're going.

Killed in an auto accident.

⬤⬤⬤⬤ ✦✦ ⬤⬤⬤⬤

It was early morning when Jonny arrived in West Port. Planning to be there for a few days, he rented a room at the Days Inn then drove around the small town. He parked at a small restaurant and ordered breakfast. The waitress was a polite, blonde, middle-aged woman.

"Good morning, sir," she said with the expected southern draw. "What can I get you today?"

"What would you recommend?"

The waitress grinned. "You're not from here are you?" It wasn't a question.

Returning her smile, Jonny said, "How can you tell?"

Now laughing, she replied, "Guess it's because you're so tall."

"Oh that. I thought it might have been my accent."

"That helped a little bit. We have a lot of tourists all year round from up north, down south, and a bunch from other countries. Anyway, my name is Nancy. I suggest you have one of our famous omelets. Our cook Benny makes the best in Kentucky."

"Benny's omelet it will be then. By the way, do you know Roger Waylon and his wife Helen?"

"My goodness, everybody knows them. In fact, everybody knows everybody here in West Port, this being a small, friendly town."

"I met them on the way here. I think they were visiting family in Ohio. Roger suggested I visit your lovely town."

Nancy stepped back in false surprise. "That would be Waylon. If you call him Roger he gets kinda cranky."

"His wife mentioned that, but I forgot. I believe he works at the military museum."

"The museum? Well, that would be a few blocks away on Elm Street. That's where you're going to find him. He's there every day, all day. Except for Sunday that is. He's in church then."

After an omelet, fried shredded potatoes, and two cups of coffee, Jonny waved at Nancy for his check. "Now which way do I go to get to Elm Street?"

Nancy gave him directions, then added, "Careful, you go too far and you end up in the Ohio River. And thanks for the tip, not many leave five dollars. Be sure you come back again."

⟞⟝ ✦ ✦ ⟞⟝

The Military Museum's huge tower with WEST PORT MUSEUM posted on it and a civil war cannon protecting it was easy to find. Inside was just as majestic as outside of the building. Although it was early in the morning, it was packed with visitors coming and going. Jonny asked one of the vendors where he would find Mister Waylon.

"Who knows," she said with a laugh. "He could be anywhere. Your best bet is to follow the crowd. If there's a crowd, you'll find Waylon leading it."

Following the vendor's direction, he found Waylon preaching to a group of visitors. Jonny worked his way to the front of the crowd. Recognizing Jonny he motioned to a young man. "Folks I enjoyed sharing what little I know with you, but now I'll turn you over to David. He knows everything I know because I taught him everything he knows." The crowd laughed as Waylon motioned to Jonny to follow him.

"Dang it if it ain't Mister Jim."

"I warned you I might come by here."

"I'm glad to see you, and I know Helen will be too. She thought you were a nice man. Look, join the group being educated for now, then come up to the second floor to my office. You can't miss it, it says *WAYLON* on it in big letters."

"I don't want to keep you from your job, so I'll on David's tour and see you later if that's okay."

"Tell ya what. Come to my house this evening for dinner. It's not far from here, and don't say no," he said as he jotted down his address. "Helen will tear me apart if you don't."

Jonny spent the rest of the day walking the streets that held centuries of history and catching up on his sleep.

❖ ❖

Dinner consisted of fried chicken, southern mashed potatoes, and cornbread. While Helen cleaned up the table, Jonny and Waylon headed for the living room where Jonny learned a lot about the small town's history.

"West Port is one of the oldest towns in Kentucky. It started out being much of nothing. You can attribute that to the Indian attacks. Anyway, our ancestors finally got through that and it became a permanent settlement thanks a lot to a Virginia named James Young. They named a bridge after him-"

"And don't forget the river walk up the Ohio River," Helen said as she joined them.

"Ya, that too. Anyway, they gradually grew us into a real town with a lot of jobs. One of them was the sugar refinery and the old salt mines-"

"Don't forget the boat building, Waylon. It brings a lot to the town."

"I didn't forget your father's boat-building thing, Helen, I just hadn't got to it yet. I was about to tell Jim he would likely find a job there if he wanted to stay here."

"It's hard work but pays pretty good," Helen added. "And there's a motel close to it."

Jonny stayed, and he found a job at the boat factory. It was hard work, totally different from the desk job he had in the past, but he liked the change. It lasted six months then August came. His new life was about end. He had his last breakfast at Nancy's restaurant and his last dinner with the Waylons.

"Why are you leaving, Jim?" Waylon asked. "They like you at the boat company. Goodness knows Nancy likes seeing you every morning-"

Helen cut him off. "Nancy *loves* seeing him, Waylon. I was hoping something would come of that. I know she was too."

"I appreciate all you have done for me," Jonny said as he put his hand on Helen's. "But I've got something I have to do back in New York, and there's a chance I won't be able to come back."

Little did Jonny know how right he was.

CHAPTER 19

Mathew Brookdale had just finished three days on the road delivering his company's variety of items to fifty stores in Ohio. His job kept him on the road six days out of seven. Two years ago, he appreciated these hours–more time alone, more time to think, less time to have to be social. He just pulled his eighteen-wheeler up to the dock when his cell phone rang. "This is Matt." After that, he just listened.

After hanging up, he stretched then coughed. The cough was followed by a gobbet of blood-tainted sputum. When this began a year ago, he blamed his weight loss, fatigue, cough, and bloody sputum on bouncing hours after hours, day after day, in Brighton Company's semi-truck. It didn't take long for him to realize that he was passing blame instead of facing the truth. What he heard in the surprise phone call made him realize he had to deal with his past failures with the little time he had left. After wiping the blood from his mouth with the back of his hand, he went into the company office.

"How was your trip, Matt?" the potbellied man behind the desk asked.

"'Bout the same, Sam. But this job is getting to be punishing. I need another job . . . maybe your job," he said with a laugh.

"Nah! You wouldn't want a job like mine. Just sitting down and stamping documents takes a lazy man, not someone who was made for the open plains."

Matt moaned as he tossed a stack of receipts on the desk. "You're right. I wouldn't last a week doing paperwork." When he stood to leave, he turned back to Sam. "Sam, I need a week or two off the road."

"Business is picking up, Matt. I don't think the boss will give you time off right now."

"I've got a lot of vacation time built up."

"Can't you wait until business slows down?"

"No! I've got some medical issues that can't wait."

"Sounds important."

"Yeah, it is. I've been worrying about these bloody coughs too long."

"You think you're worried, just get married, then you'll really have something to worry about."

Matt laughed. "It's Nancy who should be doing all the worrying."

"Ya, I know. But that's what marriage's for . . . someone to worry about you. Try it. Get yourself a wife," Sam said as he finished his paperwork.

"Been there. Didn't last long."

"Divorce?"

Matt's cough brought up blood-tainted sputum again. "No. She was a good woman who put up with me for four years."

"Another woman? That can kill a marriage."

"Nothing like that. I just wasn't the home-style type, at least not then. I changed, but it was too late, she passed on . . . cancer of some type. I regret being the man I was then."

"Gosh, what kind of man were you then?"

Matt ignored the question. "How long you been married?"

"Come next June, it'll be forty years of jail time. Anyway, vacation time off this time of year is out of the question."

"Sam, I need it!"

Sam rubbed his chin for a minute, cleared his throat, and pointed a finger at Matt. "Well, you do have a lot of sick time built up, and looking at what you cough up, you might be coming down with something. I think I can get him to give you one or two weeks of sick leave."

"Thanks, Sam. If it's okay, I'll start tomorrow. By the way, my truck is on its last leg. Any chance I could use one of the company's vans?"

"Take the one out front," Sam said as he tossed the keys. "Just make sure it comes back in as good shape as it left."

"You know me, Sam, and thanks."

"That's what bothers me, Matt . . . I know you."

⊰⊱ ◈ ◈ ⊰⊱

It was dark when Matt settled down in the Economy Motel on the east side of the Bronx. Luxury was the last thing he cared about. After a clean shave and a *do-it-yourself* haircut, he looked in the smudged mirror. He sighed at the man he saw. Weight loss was evident, more so in his pale face. He hardly recognized Mathew Brookdale. That worked for him. He started to go over his plan, but fatigue sent him into a deep sleep. Eight hours later, barking dogs woke him.

After a quick shower, he went to the closest fast-food restaurant, gobbled down eggs and bacon held together with a toasted biscuit. Then he went to a liquor store and bought a bottle of whiskey. It had been a long time since needed a boost of alcohol to support his bravery. It took several glasses of whiskey to calm his nerves enough to dial the number Paulie gave him. An angry voice answered.

"Hello!"

"Is this Don Ferrari's residence?"

Ferrari slammed the phone down. A minute later, it rang again. "Who the hell is calling me at my home at this time of the morning?"

"You don't know me, but my name is Mathew Brookdale, Mister Ferrari. I promise if you give me just a minute or two, you will want to hear more."

"A minute is all you have before I hang up again."

"You're looking for someone . . . someone I know." Having Ferrari's attention, he continued. "I can't say more over the phone. You never know when your phone has been bugged. Let me come to you."

"Bugged or not, you need to tell me more than that before I'll meet with you."

"It has to do with *company books* and the Mexico thing!"

An hour later, Matt was being frisked and escorted to Ferrari's home office. Once inside, Ferrari, in his bathroom robe, entered the room with a bottle and two glasses. "You have five minutes to make your speech, Mister Brookdale," he said as he filled the glasses with bourbon. "And it better be a meaningful speech. If it's not, this might be the last drink you ever have."

Matt took a deep drink hoping it would slow his pounding heart. "I believe you and *others* are eager to find Jonny Milano. I said I could help you find him, but--"

"But?"

"I may have misled you, Mister Ferrari. I said I knew Jonny Milano, but I don't. But I can help you find him."

Eyes narrowed, face flushing, Ferrari set his glass down. "I don't like conversations that have a lot of *buts* in it, Mister Brookdale. You need to put the *buts* away and tell me just what you have for me and why you're here."

"I'm here to warn you about Don Vallario."

Ferrari got out of his chair and leaned over his desk. "Warn me? Warn me about what?"

"It's a long story, much of which you might or might not know."

Ferrari was still standing, but now eye to eye, finger-pointing in his Matt's face. "I don't know what game you're playing, but I think you're either stupid or mentally deranged to make such a statement. I'm warning you now . . . you're walking on thin ice, so be careful . . . very careful about what you say next."

"Sometimes I'm told I'm a bit deranged, but never stupid. I wouldn't be here if I didn't have information that would be valuable to you. It's a long story, so you might want to sit back down."

Ferrari was taken back by the change in Matt's tone and lack of fear. He leaned back into his chair in response to all he heard. "You've said a lot, but you left out one thing . . . Jonny Milano."

"I'm very good at tracking people down. Usually, I charge a lot, but you can consider it a personal favor. You have nothing to lose."

Ferrari had a gut feeling, *this man isn't crazy or stupid.*

Seeing that he now had Ferrari's attention, Matt continued. "All of this shit started in Mexico when Vallario sent soldiers to kill Garcia. As you know, his plan backfired. You can blame De Luca, for that. Whatever happened down there affected Jonny Milano."

"Yeah, I know. But how are Vallario or Milano threats to me?"

Matt was now feeling he owned the conversation. "I'm getting to that. Milano lost a friend then a girlfriend because of Vallario's poor judgment. That's why you're sitting here instead of De Luca. An agreeable outcome most believe, but there were results not so agreeable; dead men, one dead Don, and another in Milano's sight."

"So you think Milano is coming for me, too?"

"No. He has no gripe with you. It's Vallario he wants. Did you know he's was a Navy Seal?"

"How does that come into the picture?"

"Well, it doesn't other than knowing he is capable of a lot of things . . . bombs and such. My source believes he was responsible for Garcia's death. But that doesn't have any effect on anything now."

"Get to the point! How am I involved in this idiotic puzzle?"

"To make a long story short, Jonny stole company books that are devastating to Vallario's *business.*

"And that is supposed to concern me?"

"Indirectly it does. Jonny couldn't get to Vallario, so he gave the feds what they wanted–Vallario's books. They have them now, and they are going to use them to put Vallario behind bars."

"None of this is my concern. Let Vallario do his time. That's--"

"You need to be concerned. Vallario is making a deal with the feds–testifying against you and other Dons. In return, he gets shorter prison time."

"How do you know all of this?"

"You have contacts; I have contacts."

"So that's how he's a threat to me!"

"You see it now? It's not *if* the feds get Vallario, it's a matter of *when.* That's all I have to say. How you deal with this is your problem."

"So what do you get out of this?"

"Nothing . . . now, but maybe I'll need a favor someday and you can help me."

"Yes. I owe you, Mister Brookdale. As for Vallario, I don't think he'll ever get to the feds."

CHAPTER 20

J onny attempted to visit Carlene's grave several times over the past year, but each time paranoia crept in . . . there was always a chance someone might be watching the grave. Two months ago, he stopped coming. However, he made sure a bouquet was placed there every week. Fear or not, he could not miss visiting her today; it was a year since she died.

"Carlene, it's me," Jonny muttered as he knelt in front of the grave's granite stone. "I know I haven't been here for a while, but things just keep popping up, but I had to come today since it's been a year since . . ." he could never say the words, *you died*. "A year since . . . *my life changed*. Anyway, I'm here and I brought you roses . . . white roses . . . the kind you like," he said as he replaced the dried flowers from his last visit with the fresh bouquet. After a brief prayer, he touched the stone. "I'm sorry . . . so sorry. I know I can't change anything, but--" He stopped when he heard footsteps behind him.

"Jonny B! I almost didn't recognize you with that beard and long hair, but who else would be here but you?"

Jonny didn't need to turn around. He recognized the three-hundred-pound, six-foot-four man's gruff voice. "Durand! You must be a mind reader."

"Not really. The Dons figured you would come here eventually, so they had someone come by occasionally. I saw you once or twice, but there was always someone around. That was pretty smart of you. I came close a couple of months ago when the place was empty . . . except for its permanent residents, that is," he laughed, "but a funeral came out of nowhere. . . not very polite of them. Again, I missed you. But I'm patient. I figured sooner or later you would be here alone."

"I guess today is your lucky day."

"Too bad it's not yours," Durand said.

"If it's all about the books, you're a bit late."

Durand laughed. "If it was just about the books, I wouldn't be here. We know you or your sweetheart sent them to the feds. Did you think the Dons would just forget about that? Bad move on your part."

"My mistake was thinking all of you would be behind bars by now."

"Thanks to Don Ferrari's fed connections, we're still here."

"Who?"

"Don Niccolo Ferrari. That's right, you wouldn't know him. He replaced De Luca. I know you remember him. After all, you killed him. Personally, that doesn't bother me. One less Don, one more Don, I still get paid. Unfortunately for you, this is one of the duties I do get paid for," then he bent over and whispered to Jonny. "To be honest, Jony B, I would have done you for nothing. You know, with your sweety resting in peace there, keeping the books could have been your salvation. But just out of curiosity, did you send them to the feds, or did she?"

"Does it matter who did?" Jonny said. "Anyway, that's something you can wonder about."

A foot kicking into Jonny's back. "Don't underestimate me. I'm not as dumb as people think I am. I know things."

"Okay. This is a bit complicated, so listen closely," Jonny said. "With the books hidden, I might have been safer, but so would Vallario and the other Dons." Pointing to the headstone, he continued. "When she died, all of the chips were off the table. There was nothing else the mob could do to me, but there was a lot I could do to them. By sending the books to the FBI, eventually, their reign would end and all of you assholes would be behind bars."

Durand laughed. "If you were as smart as everybody thought you were, why am I here?"

"There's always a seat at the table for a psychopath. I guess the new Don realized that, too."

"There you go with the big words. But I'm smart, too. And Don Ferrari is pretty smart. He knows he needs me. Who else could have taken care of Vallario? Not that pussy Paulie. Not you, the college boy. Because of me, Vallario never got to testify against any of the other Dons. Don Ferrari was smart, he didn't break the rule, you know the one that says *Don don't kill another Don*. Well, technically, the rule was bent a little since he had me do it. The only thing left was to see that you got punished. That would send a message to all the flunkeys who are working me to death . . . no pun intended."

"I hate to say it, but I owe you. Books or no books, either way, I was a mark, but I can live . . . or die with Vallario's demise."

"Demise? Another fancy word, but I know what it means. You think you're pretty smart, don't you, but you're not. You are about to be *demised*, but it didn't have to end this way. You had a chance when you had something to trade, but you threw it away. Now you got nothing."

"It's never been about me. It's about her." After a long, deep breath, Jonny turned to Durand. "Tell me one thing. Who killed her, and why?"

"That's two things, Jonny B. But I feel generous today, so I'll tell you the *why*. To the Dons, killing you is a matter of honor. You caused them a lot of headaches, so they were gonna make you an example and send the message to everybody that no one walks away from the *business*. Since they couldn't reach you, taking away the only thing you loved was the next best thing. As for the *who*, the honor went to me, but she was killed in a car accident before I could get to her. I was disappointed."

"Disappointed?"

"Yeah. If I had done the job, I would be the runner-up for your job. Maybe not the accountant part, but I'd be the *negotiator*."

"I can't see you as a negotiator."

"There are other ways to negotiate besides the soft, baby talk you use," the giant said. "As for her, she's gone. But, you're good-looking; there are other broads in town that would have cuddled up with you. Maybe it's still not too late for you to catch one of them."

"The gun you're pointing at me says something different."

"You can't negotiate with a gun, but you might be able to negotiate with me. Ain't negotiation your strong suit? We can start with you telling me where the money you took is hidden. Once I get the money, I could tell Vallario that I *took care of you.* Then you would be free to find another sweetheart somewhere and get on with your life."

"Since she's gone, I don't have a life."

"Sorry about that, Jonny," the mobster said with a laugh, "but taking my offer is your only way out of this mess. Otherwise, you'll end up in hell,".

"I'm not afraid of going to hell . . . I've already been there."

Durand pushed the gun barrel against Jonny's head. "Since we don't have anything else to talk about, let's just get this out of the way," he said in an indifferent tone, "Just for old times, I'll make it fast and--"

The next sound Jonny heard was a gunshot followed by a deep voice. "It's a good thing I was around."

Recognizing Paulie's voice, Jonny continued staring at the grave. "It looks like everyone's trying to get the credit for killing me, but I didn't think you would be one of them. But I'll be just as dead regardless of who pulls the trigger."

"What if you had another option instead of dying?"

"Options like giving you the money I took? I already dumped that offer. Or are you going to be satisfied with just the bounty money?"

"I'm not interested in your money," Paulie replied. "But I do want to give you an offer."

"I already had an offer, but I passed on it. Between the FBI and a mafia hitman. All the other options I see result in either prison or death. Humm, let's see, prison or a bullet. Excuse me if I don't like either of them."

"No prison! No bullet," Paulie said, but you still die."

The third *offer* Paulie was given was confusing. "I guess it doesn't matter how I die, I'm still dead."

Paulie nodded. "Maybe dead to the rest of the world."

"Enough of the riddles. Just do what you came here to do."

"I'm trying to do that, Jonny."

"Nothing kept you from shooting Frenchie Durand, one of your cohorts. So what's keeping you now?"

"Things are more complicated than you know," Paulie said.

"Then simplify them for me."

"I'll do my best," Paulie said. "I'll start with Vallario's plan to use Miss Sabella as a pawn to get you to send the books back. He had Durand track her down. Once he found her, she agreed to meet him with the books, but she never showed up. Durand would pay for that later. What bothered Vallario most was that Durand's screw-up caused him to lose the only thing he thought would get you to return the books, Miss Sabella. Although Vallario's books made a strong case against him and not so much against the others, the other Dons decided they couldn't take the risk. Something had to be done."

"What happened to their *All for One* policy?"

Paulie laughed. "It quickly evaporated when the other Dons focused on the possibility that the books could eventually get into the hands of the FBI, and Vallario would be indicted. Knowing him, they were concerned he would agree to testify against them in exchange for a shorter jail sentence. So they met and decided that he had created too many problems for himself and the other *families*. You made their concerns even bigger when they learned that the feds got hold of the books."

"You have it wrong," Jonny said. "The Mob created the problem." He hit the ground with his fist and shouted, "Books or not, they planned to kill me and her. The car *accident* wasn't an *accident*. It was Vallario's way of getting her out of the way."

"No. That's--"

"What do you mean, *no*? She's dead!"

"It's like I said, Jonny, it's complicated. Life is complicated."

"Being dead is not complicated. What is complicated is how you know all of this and how you knew I would be here."

"I'll make things clear, Jonny. I'm with the FBI."

"The FBI? So the feds are joining up with a mafia soldier now. So much for their integrity," Jonny said mockingly.

Paulie kneeled on the well-kept ground next to Jonny. "I'm not just with the FBI, Jonny, I am the FBI. My real name is Paul Michele, FBI Agent, Paul Michele, but my friends still call *Paulie*."

Jonny looked surprised. "FBI? You with the feds? It can't get any more complicated than that."

"Let me make it less complicated," Paulie said. "I infiltrated the mafia several years ago."

"It's not like Vallario to make such a mistake."

"He was cautious at first, but he kept me around even when I avoided doing the company's *special* business, other than killing someone with blanks? Did you ever wonder why?"

"He did a lot of things I wondered about, but everyone wondered why he would keep someone who was . . . what is the word? Oh, yeah, incompetent."

Paulie laughed. "That was the role I played. But that allowed me to hear a lot and learn a lot. He had Durand keep an eye on me. While he was doing that, I was keeping an eye on him. One of the things I learned was, although you did some things that seemed to be out of your character, you were not the typical Vallario *employee*. As far as I know, you never stepped over the line. That troubled Vallario a bit, but like needing me, he needed you."

All he needed was someone who could count and correct *off the record expenditures* without asking any questions," Jonny said. "But it didn't hurt that my dad was on his payroll."

Paulie nodded. "I quess your right about that, but everything changed when your father was out of the picture. Your anger over the Mexican issue made you a liability rather than an asset. You had to pay, but by the time Vallario made that decision, you were out of his reach. But he still had Miss Sabella. He sent Durand to find out if she knew where the books were, and if possible find out where you disappeared to. That put her in danger."

"She didn't know where the books were," Jonny said. "And she didn't know where I was."

"Durand didn't know that. Even if he did, it wouldn't have mattered. Sure, getting the books or you wouldn't have saved her. Books or not, to him she was just an inconvenience that he could have fun with then kill her. I couldn't let that happen, so I told her, regardless of what Durand promised, not to let him know where she was."

"She was a smart girl," Jonny said. "She would have figured that out herself."

"Yes, she was smart. Still, it would be just a matter of time before Durand found her," Paulie said. "He never gives up. But you know that, too. So, instead of letting her stay at her home, I told her to make him think she had the books and would bring them to him, but only if they met in a public place where she felt safe."

"And the dumbass agreed?

Paulie nodded. "I figured he would if he thought it would be the fastest way to get the books."

"You didn't believe he would forget everything once he had the books, did you?"

Paulie took a deep breath as he continued. "Knowing the bastard, I knew he wouldn't stop until he found her . . . and eventually you. Our plan was for her to appease him enough to buy time for her to come to us. I don't think she trusted us either and she hesitated at first."

"So she did die in the car accident on her way to you?" Jonny asked with tears building up in his eyes. "I guess it doesn't matter how she died, she would still be alive if she wasn't running away from him."

"Yes and no." Seeing Jonny's confusion, he put his hand on Jonny's shoulder. "Jonny, things are not always the way they look."

Jonny laughed. "Your right about that. I never should have taken the damn books. That cost me more than I realized." After a minute of silence, he nodded and continued, now in a somber tone. "At least there was some justice."

"Justice?" Paulie asked.

"If this jerk was telling the truth about him killing Vallario, I consider that some justice."

"We don't know for sure by who or how, but he's right about Vallario being taken care of," Paulie said. "But the who and how doesn't matter. What does matter is that we have Vallario's books. Although he's not around anymore, we can use them against the other Dons."

"Vallario might be dead, but the other Dons aren't," Jonny said as he continued to stare at the grave. "You don't know them. They probably think I killed Vallario and they know I killed De Luca and that I sent the books to you. Despite all of your promises, giving me a new name won't stop them. They have ways of finding anyone if they want to find them. And believe me, I'm someone they want to find."

"We have our ways, too, Jonny," Paulie said.

"Just tell me what you can do. Since it's my life you're talking about, I have a right to know."

"Things like planting your wallet and other personal items in this jerk's pocket," Paulie said as he pointed to Durand lying spread out on the ground. "Then making a news statement saying *One of the Mobster's boys, Jonny Milano, is no longer around.* In the meantime, we take you . . . the, *him* you." Paulie pointed to Durand again, "To one of our friendly morticians where he'll have a closed casket ceremony then planted next to the grave in front of you."

"I don't want him next to her. Why not just burn the jerk?"

"We could do that, but we want something more than a newspaper obituary. We want something people can see, something that reminds them that Jonny Milano is dead. Trust us, we like doing complicated things. Just ask the man standing over there," Paulie said as he pointed to a tall man with a walking cane two graves away.

The stranger waved a hand then walked over to Jonny. "Why are you moaning over an empty grave?"

His eyes widened. Although he did not recognize the man, he recognized the voice. "DAD!

Mario Milano smiled and hugged his son. "I'm surprised you would recognize a dead man, especially one with a beard."

"Why? How? Everyone thought you were dead."

"I was, but this man resurrected me as Mister Mathew Brookdale. The why? No one leaves the Mafia. But like you, I wanted out. And you're right, changing your name and disappearing doesn't last long if the Mafia wants to find you. But, if you're dead nobody looks for you. The how is the same way the FBI protected me," Mario said as he held his son an arm's length away, "but you have to understand something."

Jonny was confused. "What?"

A tear dribbled down Mario's cheek as he said, "Once Jonny Milano is dead, he has to remain dead. That means we cannot see each other again."

Jonny was stunned. "But--"

Paulie answered him. "That's the FBI's rules to ensure both of your safety."

"I understand," Jonny said as he turned back to the granite monument. "But what do you mean, by an *empty grave?*"

Then Mario said the last thing he would say to his son. "Go to this address, and you'll see what I mean."

"He's right," Paulie added. "But you might not recognize the resident after our cosmetic workup."

After Jonny Milano traded his old life for a new one, he headed south. The twelve-hour drive to Clayton was filled with anger, remorse, and redemption. But, as he stood in front of 324 Sea Brook Lane, Clayton, Georgia, he had only one thing in mind. After staring at the door for several anxious minutes, he smiled. When he rang the doorbell, a blue-eyed blonde opened the door. With tears running down her cheeks, she wrapped her arms around him and said, "I thought you'd never get here, Jonny."

"I'm sorry Miss, but you have the wrong man. My name is John, John Randell."

THE END

Printed in the United States
by Baker & Taylor Publisher Services